THE BACHELOR EARL

DARCY BURKE

THE BACHELOR EARL

For two years following the death of her beloved husband, Eugenia, the Dowager Duchess of Kendal has grieved and kept to herself. Her cousin is hosting a house party and has persuaded Genie to attend—it's the perfect opportunity to emerge from mourning. Genie is looking forward to seeing old friends but is shocked when she learns the true purpose of the occasion: to match widowed ladies with widowed and unmarried gentlemen.

Once infatuated with a young Eugenia Aldwick, Edmund Holt, Earl of Satterfield is thrilled when Genie arrives at the matchmaking house party. Mutual attraction sparks between them immediately, however he is in need of a wife who can provide an heir and she is unable to do so. Genie would also dearly love to be a mother after losing her daughter several years before. Can they embrace a second chance at love or will the demands of his title and the pull of her maternal heart prove too strong to ignore?

Want to share your love of my books with like-minded readers? Want to hang with me and get inside scoop? Then don't miss my exclusive Facebook groups!

Darcy's Duchesses for historical readers
Burke's Book Lovers for contemporary readers

The Bachelor Earl
and Bonus Material from The Untouchables
Copyright © 2020 Darcy Burke
All rights reserved.

ISBN: 9781637260029

Book Design: © Darcy Burke.
Book Cover Design: © The Midnight Muse.
Cover Image: © Period Images.
Cover Image: © Annie Ray/Passion Pages.
Darcy Burke Font Design: © Carrie Divine/Seductive Designs
Editing: Linda Ingmanson.

❧ Created with Vellum

CHAPTER 1

October 1803

The sky had grown increasingly darker as they neared the Blickton estate, and not because night was falling. A fat raindrop hit the window of Eugenia St. John's coach as they turned up the drive toward the manor house. Trees dressed in gold and orange swayed in the wind, and Genie wondered how many leaves would be left on the branches come tomorrow.

Pity, for she loved the glorious colors of autumn. As had her dear husband. The familiar ache in her chest had lessened gradually over the past two years since his death, but it was still there. She wondered if it would always be. At least now when she thought of him, she smiled, and any tears she shed were due to fond memories instead of grief.

The house finally came into view, its pale stone Palladian structure rising into the blackening sky. Built less than a hundred years ago, Blickton was not as grand as Lakemoor, but then few estates were. Her husband, the Duke of Kendal, had kept Lakemoor and its land in excellent condition, and his son and heir was continuing that commitment, which Genie observed from the dower house.

The coach came to a stop in front of the door, and a footman rushed out with an umbrella. The rain began to fall in earnest as Genie stepped from the coach and hurried inside, her maid trailing behind.

"Welcome, Your Grace," the butler greeted her. "The guests are gathered in the drawing room."

Genie might have asked to go to her room first to change out of her traveling costume, but the hostess, her cousin Lady Cosford, bustled into the cavernous entry hall, her shoes tapping on the marble floor.

"Genie, you're here at last! Come and meet the rest of the guests. I promise you can retire after a short introduction." Cecilia smiled broadly, her sherry-brown eyes sparkling. She was always effusively cheerful. Genie had been particularly grateful for that trait after her husband had died.

It was because Cecilia had been so supportive and wonderful that Genie had agreed to come to her house party. The event would be her first major social occasion since Jerome's death.

Genie summoned a smile. "Of course." She removed her hat and gloves and handed them to her maid.

Cecilia linked her arm with Genie's and swept her through several rooms until they reached the large drawing room that overlooked the vast parkland of the Blickton estate. "Everyone, please welcome the Dowager Duchess of Kendal!"

Dowager. Genie bristled inwardly at that title. She'd never thought to be a widow at the age of forty-two.

Surveying the room, she recognized only a handful of faces. She estimated there were twenty or so people in attendance. It also seemed at first glance that there was a rather equal ratio of men and women.

"Welcome, Genie!" One of the people Genie knew came forward, smiling brightly, her pale blue eyes sparkling with delight. Lady Bradford, a fellow widow, had been a dear friend.

Had been. Because Genie had isolated herself at her dower house at Lakemoor for the past two years.

Genie smiled warmly, genuinely glad to see Letitia. "I'm so pleased to see you, Lettie."

"And I you." She lowered her voice as she moved closer so that only Genie could hear. "I was afraid you wouldn't come."

"I nearly didn't," Genie whispered, surprising herself at the disclosure.

"Now that everyone is here," Cecilia said, "let us have proper introductions. We'll go around the room, and when it's your turn, say your name and something about yourself."

"What should we say?" one gentleman asked, his brow arching.

Cecilia lifted a shoulder. "Whatever you choose. Though perhaps refrain from something so mundane as how many children you have or what you ate for breakfast. I'll start. I'm Lady Cosford, your hostess, and I sleep with the window open all year round."

"Even on a day like this?" a lady asked from the other side of the room.

"*Especially* on a day like this. I love the smell of the rain." Cecilia turned her head to the gentleman on her left. "Your turn, Mr. Sterling."

Since Genie stood on Cecilia's right, she would go last. Another quick review of the room said this was going to take forever. Genie exhaled softly.

Slightly taller than average, Mr. Sterling possessed a charming smile and dark blue eyes that crinkled at the corners, giving the impression he was a

man of good humor. "Then I shouldn't start by ex-
tolling the virtues and follies of my four children."
This was met with laughter and shouts of "No!" from
a few gentlemen, followed by more laughter.

"All right, then," Mr. Sterling said, stifling his own
chuckle. "I keep a hothouse with exotic flowers."

"Ooh, that sounds lovely," said the woman
standing to his left. She took her turn next, and so
the game—for that was what it seemed to be—continued around the room. Somewhere across the
circle from Genie, she began to lose focus, her brain
and body tired from the journey even though she
simply rode in a carriage. What was it about travel
that was so exhausting?

The sharp point of Cecilia's elbow jolted Genie
from her reverie. "Say that again, Lord Satterfield?"
Cecilia said, fluttering her lashes.

"I said my favorite color is purple."

Cecilia shot Genie an arch look that was clearly
meant to communicate something. Then her lips
pursed, and she dipped her gaze to Genie's traveling
costume. Which was…purple.

So? Genie glanced about and quickly registered
that she was the only one in purple. She looked
across the room and saw Lord Satterfield—that was
his name, wasn't it?—staring straight at her. Heat
bloomed in Genie's chest and spread outward,
warming her blood and flushing her skin. It wasn't
just that he was staring at her. It was the way he was
staring—he had the most arresting eyes, dark like a
black coffee, with what should have been feminine
lashes but that looked wholly perfect on him. He
looked at her as if he simply couldn't tear his attention away.

But then he did, as the game continued. Genie let
out her breath, and only then did she realize she'd
been holding it. She spent the next several minutes

thinking about why she'd felt that sudden flash of fever. Perhaps she was becoming ill.

At last, it was almost her turn. She had no idea what she was going to say. Why hadn't she spent this time thinking of something witty or at least interesting? Probably because she was the least interesting person she knew. Or so it seemed that was what she'd become.

Cecilia looked at her encouragingly. "It's your turn," she whispered.

"I'm..." Genie croaked. She coughed gently. "I'm the Dowager Duchess of Kendal, but then Cec—Lady Cosford already told you that. This is my first house party in some time. I, ah, like to dance." How perfectly boring and predictable.

"Excellent, for there will be plenty of dancing!" Cecilia said, clapping her hands together. "Lovely, now we all know one another. We'll adjourn shortly so that those who wish to retire for a time may do so before we gather for dinner. We'll meet here at half six and then proceed to the dining room at seven. After dinner, there will be cards and dancing. Tomorrow, we have entertainments planned, including a picnic and a walk to the River Swift." She looked behind her toward the doorway and frowned. "I do wonder where Cosford has taken off to." She smiled brightly. "Ah well, he'll be here soon, I imagine. If you haven't yet been to your room, a footman will escort you. And here are some refreshments!"

Several footmen entered bearing trays of food and drink. Genie's stomach growled softly in response, and she dearly hoped no one heard it. As tired as she was, apparently she was even hungrier.

The food—sandwiches, biscuits, and cakes—was set on a table situated in one corner of the room while the drinks went to another table in another corner. Genie went straight toward the food, but was almost immediately intercepted by the first gentleman who'd spoken, Mr. Sterling.

"This is my first house party in some time too," he said with a half smile. "I've just come out of mourning."

"Oh, I'm so sorry." Genie realized there hadn't been a Mrs. Sterling. At least that she'd heard of. But then her attention had waned. Still, she'd caught many names, and wouldn't his wife have been standing next to him?

Except there is no wife.

Genie thought back to the game. Had there been *any* wives? Rather, had there been any married couples? Save their hosts, of course. No, she didn't think there were. How peculiar.

"I know you understand," Mr. Sterling said. "It's not easy to carry on after losing one's spouse. Particularly with children. Do you have children?"

There was always a deep ache when someone asked that question. Genie had long ago learned to ignore it, bury it, and once in a while indulge it. Now was not that time.

"Just my stepson, but he is twenty-four and quite capable of managing on his own." Mostly. He still allowed her to mother him, and for that, she was grateful. He'd taken his father's death perhaps even harder than Genie. He'd certainly spent the last two years proving he would be as excellent a duke as his father had been.

"Right. I like to dance too. Hopefully, I'm still as spry as I was in my youth." Sterling chuckled. He looked to be around the same age as Genie, with some gray streaking his dark hair. He was attractive in a distinguished, mature way. What did that even mean? It meant she hadn't considered anyone attractive since she'd met Jerome almost twenty years ago. "I hope you'll save me one this evening?"

"Certainly." Genie's stomach made another desperate sound, much to her horror.

Sterling chuckled again. "Shall we move to the refreshments?"

"Yes, please." Genie continued toward the table, and from the corner of her eye caught Lord Satterfield watching her.

You find him *attractive.*

Yes, she did. Fine. So she hadn't found anyone attractive *except* Lord Satterfield since Jerome.

Heat jumped through her again as she picked up a plate and selected a few items to eat. Glancing about for somewhere safe to partake, her gaze landed on a small, and thankfully empty, seating area on the opposite side of the room.

Genie strode there with purpose, eager to satisfy her hunger and be on her way to her room to fortify herself for the evening ahead. Fortify herself? Was she going into battle?

She was being quite absurd. This was a harmless house party, meant to help her transition from mourning back to life. But what life was that exactly?

Reaching the seating area, Genie sank into a chair and took a bite of a small sandwich. The ham was deliciously smoked. She briefly closed her eyes in delight.

"Good sandwich?" The masculine voice nearly made her choke. She opened her eyes, swallowing, as she looked up.

Lord Satterfield sat down beside her. His dark eyes perused her with warm appreciation. He was broad shouldered and fit, with a handsome visage marked by a small but distinctive cleft in his chin and the sort of angular cheekbones that made them look as if they'd been sculpted. His dark hair was thinning, resulting in a wide, masculine forehead. His dearth of hair did not detract from his good looks in the slightest.

He held a glass of something, brandy perhaps, and raised it to his lips for a sip. Genie fixated on his mouth before realizing—much to her horror—that she was staring. Dropping her gaze to her plate, she finished the last of her ham sandwich.

"My brandy is delicious," he said, perhaps prompting her that she'd failed to answer his question. Because she'd been too busy staring.

Genie picked up another sandwich. "The ham is quite good. You should try it." It was a thinly veiled attempt to get him to leave. Why was she so eager for him to go? Wasn't the point of coming to the party to reestablish social connections?

Taking a deep breath, Genie summoned a smile. Then she took another bite of sandwich. This one was fowl—pheasant, she thought. It wasn't as good as the ham.

"I'm not terribly hungry," Satterfield said. "I am thirsty, however." His eyes sparked with mischief before he took another sip. "I'm trying to think if we've met before. I knew your husband, of course. We worked together in the Lords."

"Did you? Kendal was quite dedicated to reform. Are you?"

"I am indeed. Sometimes it makes me unpopular, but I don't mind. Kendal didn't either."

It felt strange to be discussing her husband, in part because "Kendal" now meant her stepson. In her mind, Titus was still Ravenglass, which had been his courtesy title, but to everyone else, he was now the duke. Genie's husband—and their time as duke and duchess—was gone.

"Is this difficult?" Satterfield asked softly.

"No." It shouldn't be. Quite enough time had

passed. "It's actually nice to speak of him, especially with someone who knew him."

"I admired him very much, actually. He offered guidance to me when I first came to the Lords—fifteen years ago or so."

"That doesn't surprise me. I often called him the Shepherd, for he was fond of guiding everyone who would allow it." Genie didn't have to summon the smile that rose to her lips this time.

Satterfield smiled with her. "What an excellent name for him. I wish I'd known to call him that."

For the first time since her arrival, Genie began to relax. Perhaps this would be just what she needed.

Satterfield studied her a moment. "I was surprised to see you here, Duchess."

Something in his tone made Genie sit up straighter, her senses tingling. "Why is that?"

"I'd heard you were in deep mourning and that you may sit out a third Season come spring."

Of course there were rumors about her. Gossip made London go round. "Well, this isn't exactly the Season," she said, feeling a trifle defensive. "It seemed just the right opportunity to dip my toe back into the sea."

Satterfield's brow creased, which only further pricked Genie's awareness. However, before she could think on his reaction further, Lord Cosford strode into the drawing room.

"I'm so pleased you are all here! Please forgive my tardiness." He looked around the assemblage until his gaze settled lovingly on Lady Cosford. After a brief moment, he readdressed the room. "As I said, I'm so pleased you are all here, because if you weren't already, I'm afraid you wouldn't have made it. The rain has washed out the road, and given the way it's pouring, it may be that way for a few days. It's a good thing you'd all planned to be here for a week!" He chortled. "In fact, you may be here longer, and I daresay you won't mind." He winked, and this was met with laughter from nearly everyone. Only nearly, because Genie wasn't sure what was funny.

"Needless to say," Lord Cosford continued, "we'll be making some adjustments to our activities." He looked to his wife once more. "I know my darling wife has alternate plans, so rest assured there will be amusements for all. Now, I think it's time I had a brandy!" He turned toward the nearest footman, then stopped. "I nearly forgot. If you haven't yet received your map, raise your hand, and Vernon will bring it to you."

Genie swallowed the rest of her second sandwich, then looked at Satterfield. "What map? If we can't go outside, why would we need a map?"

The earl cocked his head, looking at her...dubiously. Again, Genie had an odd sensation. And she was finally beginning to realize that she was missing something.

Satterfield raised his hand, and a moment later, the butler delivered a folded parchment to him. "I already have one," he said to Genie. "This one is for you. However, I take it you don't know what it's for." He frowned slightly. "Did Lady Cosford not explain the purpose of this party?"

Purpose? What purpose did a house party have aside from providing social opportunity and amusement? Genie took the map and opened the parchment. "Is this the house?" She glanced over at the earl.

"Upstairs, to be precise."

She could see that. In each bedroom was written someone's name or initials. She found hers—at least she thought DDK meant her, the Dowager Duchess of Kendal. Why on earth would they give out maps of everyone's bedrooms? Unless... No, that was too scandalous.

Genie looked around the room at the people assembled. Not one wife. Not one husband. No one was a couple, save their hosts. In fact, Genie was fairly certain every woman in attendance was a widow. What the devil kind of party was this?

Standing so quickly she upended her plate, Genie felt heat rush to her face. Before she could bend down to pick up the biscuits that had tumbled to the floor, as well as the plate, Lord Satterfield did it for her.

When he stood, he took a step closer, so that there was scarcely any space between them. Their proximity both terrified and excited her. She hadn't been this close to a man in some time. She hadn't been this close to a man who wasn't her husband *ever*.

"I'm sorry you didn't know," he said softly. "But I'm glad you're here."

Genie couldn't move. Her heart beat faster, and she wondered if he could hear it. He turned and walked away, taking her plate and biscuits with him. Which was fine since she'd quite lost her appetite.

She located Cecilia across the room, standing with her husband, and made her way quickly in that direction. "Cecilia, may I have a word?" Genie tried to keep her voice pleasant.

Cecilia turned toward her, smiling. "Of course."

"Welcome to Blickton, Duchess," Lord Cosford said cheerfully. "We're so glad you came."

Genie narrowed her eyes slightly before pinning her attention on Cecilia. "Privately, please?"

Concern flashed in Cecilia's gaze. "Certainly." She walked with Genie from the drawing room. Once they were several paces away from the doorway, she stopped and turned toward Genie. "Is there something amiss?"

Holding up the map, Genie struggled to keep her emotions in check. "What is this?" No, that wasn't the right question. Genie knew what it was. What she didn't know was *why* it was. "What is this party about?"

Pink dotted Cecilia's cheeks, validating the shock and distress Genie felt. "Oh dear, I can see you're upset. I should have told you straightaway, but I was afraid you wouldn't come."

She was damn right Genie wouldn't have come. "Everyone here is unmarried."

"Yes. Our hope was to provide an opportunity for those who are unwed and perhaps wish to be wed again to meet and establish connections."

"What sort of connections?" Genie glanced toward the paper in her hand. "*You provided a map with everyone's bedrooms.*"

The color in Cecilia's face deepened. "Ah, yes, we did. We are also providing an opportunity for more… intimate connections, should someone desire."

Genie stared at her, unthinking, for a moment. "This is mad."

"It isn't, really. Lady Greville hosted a party like this a couple of years ago, and it was a great success." Cecilia's fixed on Genie with a half smile, her eyes shining with empathy. "I actually thought of hosting it precisely for you."

"You can't think I would want to wed again. Or… anything else."

"Why not?" Cecilia's russet brows gathered together. "You're young, beautiful, intelligent. There's no reason you should be alone."

"No reason at all, except that I want to be. I'm leaving." As soon as the words left her mouth, she realized departure was impossible.

"You can't. The road—"

"Is impassable." Genie ground her teeth. "I feel as though you tricked me."

Cecilia reached out to touch Genie's hand, but

Genie stepped back. "I'm so sorry. I didn't mean to. I truly thought you would be amenable. You've always been the most cordial— even gregarious—woman."

"That doesn't mean I want to marry again. Or have an affair. I was looking forward to a house party, not...whatever this is."

"Forgive me." Cecilia's face fell, and she twisted her hands together. "This can still be just a house party for you."

Genie wasn't sure she believed that. She opened her mouth to respond, but, deciding there wasn't anything she could think to say, she simply turned on her heel and began to walk away. Thankfully, the inconceivable map would show the way to her room.

"I'll see you at dinner!" Cecilia called, her tone bursting with hope.

Again, Genie didn't respond. Because she didn't know what she was going to do.

CHAPTER 2

*E*dmund Holt, Earl of Satterfield, sipped his port as male conversation rumbled around him in the dining room. He'd spent dinner across the table from the Dowager Duchess of Kendal, or, as he remembered her from his youth, Miss Aldwick. He recalled seeing her, the daughter of a viscount and the youngest of five sisters, at one of the very first balls he'd attended at the age of twenty.

Tall, with a grace and elegance that had seemed at odds with her youth, she possessed piercing gray eyes illuminated with intelligence, she'd caught Edmund's attention immediately. But he'd been on the verge of his Grand Tour and had no intention to marry, while she'd been on the Marriage Mart—delayed a few years due to the deaths of her parents. She was two years older, a fact that hadn't bothered him the slightest then and was still inconsequential.

She'd had a wonderful laugh, and a smile that dazzled the entire ballroom. Edmund hadn't gathered the courage to ask her to dance. He'd also assumed all her dances were claimed given her popularity. For the weeks that followed until he departed, he kept a distant eye on her, watching as she had her pick of the gentlemen available that Season.

It seemed she would choose the Marquess of Raven-glass, but then his father, the Duke of Kendal, had died in an accident, and that match seemed unlikely. The next Edmund had heard—the following winter —she'd wed the new duke. It had been heralded as a love match, with Miss Aldwick waiting patiently for Kendal as he mourned his father and took his place as the duke.

That Edmund remembered all that didn't surprise him—he'd thought of her often through the years. And if someone asked him whether he'd been aware that she'd become a widow two years ago, the answer would be yes. He'd known, and something inside him had sparked. Because he'd never wed. In the past twenty years, not one woman had stirred him the way Miss Aldwick had. As an earl, he knew it was his duty to marry, to produce an heir. Even so, he hadn't been moved to do so. And Edmund was nothing if not a romantic—or so his mother would say.

She was not wrong.

It wasn't too late for Edmund to marry and have children. That was, in fact, why he'd come to this party. He'd resigned himself to the realization that it was time. But never had he expected to find Miss Aldwick—the Dowager Duchess—here. His resigna-tion had abruptly become his exceptional good for-tune. Except that she hadn't been aware that this party's purpose was matchmaking, and, more impor-tantly, she'd seemed scandalized upon finding out.

"You're awfully quiet," Cosford said, taking the empty seat next to Edmund.

Edmund hadn't even seen his host get up from the head of the table. "Just mulling the days ahead and how you'll manage to keep us all occupied indoors with this weather."

"I will hope it will dry out, but if it doesn't, be as-sured my wife will arrange plenty of activities for everyone to do." He chuckled softly. "She'd consider the party an abject failure if she did not. Actually, she'll consider it a failure if there isn't a match made." He shook his head. "I keep telling her it's unlikely, but she insists it is."

"I have to agree with your wife," Edmund said before taking another sip of port. He set the glass back on the table, keeping his fingers curled around the stem. "Whether it's to marry or find some other… connection, it seems Lady Cosford has chosen a group that wants one or the other. Surely at least one match—either temporary or permanent—will be made."

"Careful, or I'll think your temperament is as romantic as my wife's!" Cosford laughed, but quickly sobered. He lowered his voice. "I'm not certain everyone here wants to make a match. Apparently the Dowager Duchess was not too pleased upon learning the nature of the party."

"Why didn't she know beforehand?" Hadn't she received the same invitation Edmund had? Perhaps not.

Cosford swallowed a gulp of port. "Cecilia didn't think she'd come if she knew, and of all the people here, Cecilia says she needs this party the most. The dowager has been an absolute hermit since the duke died, and Cecilia worries for her cousin."

"Still, if she wasn't ready for this, keeping the truth from her seems insensitive." Edmund didn't give a whit if he insulted his host. The Dowager Duchess's upset reaction earlier was far more troubling.

"I can't disagree, but I don't get too involved with my wife's plans, particularly when it comes to her family. She'll do what she will whether I advise her against it or not." He lifted a shoulder. "Can't say I mind either. Contrary to most of our sex, I prefer a

woman who knows what she wants and does it."
There was a gleam of pride in Cosford's eyes that
made Edmund truly desire a loving marital relationship. Maybe, in addition to feeling as though he *must*
wed, he was ready to do so?

Edmund was eager to see the dowager duchess
again. Anticipation built within him as the gentlemen
took their time over their port. He would tread cautiously with her. Assuming she was even still in the
drawing room. She'd arrived just before they'd gone
in to dinner—so late that Edmund had feared she
wasn't coming.

Then she'd appeared in a beautiful lavender gown,
the gauzy material flowing into a short train behind
her as she'd glided into the room, her dark, shining
hair swept onto her head and styled with a wide
lavender ribbon while delicate curls brushed her
temples and cheeks. She'd looked beyond lovely, and
Edmund hadn't been able to keep his eyes from
finding her throughout dinner. Which hadn't been
difficult since she'd been seated directly across from
him. That had made conversation with her all but
impossible, but he'd been able to look his fill.

"Shall we adjourn to the drawing room with the
ladies?" Cosford asked, standing.

Edmund kept himself from racing out the door.
Even so, he was the second gentleman to leave the
dining room and somehow the first to enter the
drawing room.

He didn't have to look for the dowager duchess
because she was lingering near the door, as if she'd
been about to leave. Edmund thanked fortune that
she hadn't. He didn't squander a moment, moving to
speak with her.

"I hope you weren't about to retire," he said with a
gentle smile.

"I was actually. It's been a long day of travel."

"It has indeed. Would it be terrible of me to shamelessly ask you to reconsider? I'd hoped to partner you in a dance. I remember you being an excellent dancer."

Her gorgeous gray eyes sparked with surprise as her delicate sable brows pitched into a slight V. "We danced together?"

"Sadly, we did not," he said as the last of the gentlemen came into the drawing room.

She narrowed her eyes briefly. "Then how do you know I'm a good dancer?"

"You were quite the toast of your first Season. As a young buck, I was aware of all the marriageable ladies." That wasn't true at all—he'd paid attention to none but her.

A faint blush stained her cheeks, and she glanced away. "That was some time ago. I'm surprised you remember."

"Will you stay and dance?" he asked. "I understand this party isn't quite what you expected, but surely you'd enjoy dancing."

"I don't know." Everything about her tone and her demeanor, particularly the slight dip in her shoulders, screamed hesitation. "I'm not here to make a match."

"Even if you were, who's to say you'd find one?" He smiled. "What I mean is that there are no requirements, no guarantees. If you want to simply dance, then just dance."

"You don't think someone might expect…?" She didn't say what, but Edmund could guess.

"I think if someone propositions you—for anything—you should honestly tell them you aren't interested. And if someone persists, I hope you'll tell me so I can make sure they stop."

One of her brows arched. "You're offering to protect me from unwanted advances?"

"I am. Should the need arise, I would consider it my honor to intervene on your behalf."

A smile teased her lips, and Edmund's heart stalled for a moment. "That's rather scandalous on its own. But then this entire party is incredibly scandalous."

Edmund made a noise in his throat. He found Society and its rules so tiresome. "It shouldn't be. Everyone here is an adult with the intelligence and ability to make their own decisions. There are no never-before married ladies who need worry about being ruined."

"There are, however, never-before married men," she said sardonically. "What will be done to guard their reputations?" She rolled her eyes.

Edmund laughed. "That includes me. Perhaps I could count on you to protect me as well."

"What should I do, give them the cut direct? Call them out?" She shook her head. "You could have an assignation with every woman in this house, and no one would care. Well, they might care, but your reputation wouldn't suffer. Indeed, it might actually be celebrated."

He grimaced. "Not at all fair, is it?"

"No."

"Which is why this party is just a little brilliant, isn't it?" he asked in a hushed tone. He glanced around the room at the men and women gathered. "No one's reputation is at stake."

"So easy for you to say," she said. "A woman must always be on her guard, even at a party where she is expected to misbehave."

He blinked at her, straightening. "Is it misbehavior? I don't view it that way."

"Knowing you were a student of my husband, I can assume you are rather forward in your thinking —but you are an anomaly among your sex, wouldn't you agree?" She stared at him expectantly, and once again, he was struck by the depth and beauty of her gaze.

Unfortunately, he would. "I do believe that most, if not all, the gentlemen here are of a similar mind."

"I should hope so. Otherwise, none of our reputations—those of the ladies, of course—are safe." She was disappointingly correct. "I'll dance with you," she whispered.

Edmund's blood rushed as he snapped his gaze to hers. "I am honored."

"Attention, if you please," Lord Cosford called out. "Lady Cosford has an announcement." He gestured to his wife, who stood beside him.

Lady Cosford smiled up at him in appreciation before addressing the room at large. "Before we begin the dancing, I wanted to share that tomorrow after breakfast, we will have a display of talents. If you have a particular talent you'd like to perform, please see me this evening. I am sorry the weather will keep us indoors, but this will be most diverting."

"Oh dear," the dowager duchess said, drawing Edmund's attention.

He pivoted toward her. "Is something amiss?"

"I believe my cousin will want me to perform something on the pianoforte, but I haven't played in some time."

"I'm sure she won't press you." Edmund wasn't sure at all—the woman had invited her very own cousin to this party without divulging the entire truth. "And if she does, remember that I am here to protect you."

The dowager duchess laughed. The rich sound made Edmund wish he could stay in this moment forever. "How will you do that?"

"I could ensure the pianoforte isn't working tomorrow." He gave her a conspiratorial wink.

Her eyes widened, but she laughed again. "You wouldn't."

"I most certainly would."

"No, please don't. Perhaps someone else will play. Indeed, perhaps there will be enough people wanting to perform that she won't even ask me." She sounded quite hopeful.

"I plan to do so."

Surprise flickered across her face and parted her pink lips. "Will you? Not the pianoforte, I assume, since you may very well be disabling it."

He chuckled. "Not the pianoforte."

"What, then?"

He smiled at her. "You'll just have to wait and see."

The music began, and Edmund held out his hand. "Shall we dance?"

"We shall." She put her fingers on his, and the feel of her flesh against his—for no one had donned gloves after dinner—sent a wave of longing through him.

He had no idea what the next several days held in store, but he could hardly wait to find out.

CHAPTER 3

$\mathcal{F}$ollowing a respite after breakfast the next
day, everyone gathered in the ballroom,
where a dais had been set up. Two rows of ten chairs
each stood before it. On the dais was the pianoforte,
which Genie had declined to play. And Cecilia *had*
asked. She'd also graciously accepted Genie's refusal.

Genie had thoroughly enjoyed dancing last night.
So much that even if the rest of the party was a
dismal bore, she would be delighted she'd come.

It wouldn't be a bore, however, not with Lord Satterfield in attendance. He'd quite dazzled her last
night with his dancing ability as well as his conversation. He'd been witty and charming during their
dance, and afterward, when they'd spent some time
discussing their love of horses, dislike of hot weather,
and boredom with the minuet.

Caught up in her thoughts, Genie nearly ran into
Lord Satterfield as they both arrived at the second
row at the same time. She lifted her hand to her
chest. "Pardon me, I almost didn't see you. I'm afraid
I was lost in thought."

"And here I was, completely fixed on you from the
moment I entered the ballroom," he said with a smile.
"What were you thinking of?"

"Last night, actually. I was recalling your story of your disastrous minuet with—I forget whom. I think I was laughing too hard to even hear her name."

"The whom is inconsequential. No one wanted to dance with me after that." He'd told her he gave up asking anyone for the rest of that Season.

"Well, if I'd known, I would have declined your offer last night," she said saucily.

"Then you would have missed out on a sublime set, because we danced very well together. I didn't step on your foot, nor did I knock you to the ground." Both were things he'd done during the Monstrous Minuet, as he'd called it.

Genie laughed lightly as he gestured to the two open seats at the end of the row. "After you," he said.

Stepping into the row, Genie took her seat. Lord Satterfield followed suit, moving the tails of his coat as he sat. He wore a superbly tailored coat of fine dark blue wool. His cravat was almost blindingly white, particularly against the dark color of the coat.

"Will you tell me now what you plan to perform?" Genie asked.

He grinned and shook his head. "You don't have long to wait."

"Then may I at least ask if the pianoforte is functional?"

He turned slightly toward her. "Have you changed your mind about playing?"

"I have not, but I see it's on the dais, so clearly, someone intends to play. It would be a shame if it didn't work."

"I have done nothing to interfere with its functionality," Lord Satterfield said, lifting his hand to his chest.

Cecilia stepped onto the dais and faced the assembly. "I see everyone is here. Splendid. We have nine performances to enjoy. We will begin with Lord

Satterfield, who will dazzle us with his portrayal of
Hamlet in a selection from Shakespeare's mas-
terpiece."

Genie turned her head sharply to Satterfield, surprised at his choice. She didn't have time to say anything as he stood and made his way to the dais.

He helped Cecilia down, then stepped up. "Thank
you, Lady Cosford. As she said, I shall perform a
piece from *Hamlet*. Act 3, Scene 1, to be specific."

The room instantly quieted as he turned and presented his back. Genie loved Shakespeare, and this
soliloquy was one of her favorite passages. She edged
forward in her chair, expecting him to turn around
and begin.

But he kept his back to them as he began to speak,
his voice deep and slow.

> To be, or not to be? That is the
>   question—

Then he turned, but only partially. She studied his
profile, her gaze lingering on the masculine cut of his
jaw. He lifted his right hand.

> Whether 'tis nobler in the mind to
>   suffer
> The slings and arrows of outrageous
>   fortune,
> Or to take arms against a sea of
>   troubles,

He turned fully toward them, dropping his hand
back to his side, his voice strong and steady, his gaze
fixed somewhere beyond where they sat. Genie realized she held her breath and forced herself to
exhale.

And, by opposing, end them? To die, to
    sleep—
No more—and by a sleep to say we end
The heartache and the thousand natural
    shocks
That flesh is heir to—'tis a con-
    summation
Devoutly to be wished! To die, to sleep.

To sleep, perchance to dream—ay,
    there's the rub,

His head shifted slightly, and his eye twitched.

For in that sleep of death what dreams
    may come
When we have shuffled off this mortal
    coil,
Must give us pause. There's the respect
That makes calamity of so long life.

His forehead creased as he went silent. For a fleeting moment, Genie wondered if he'd forgotten the rest. But no, this was too beautiful, too intentional. She held her breath again until he continued. Then his voice returned, more stirring and seductive than before.

For who would bear the whips and
    scorns of time,
Th' oppressor's wrong, the proud man's
    contumely,
The pangs of despised love, the law's
    delay,
The insolence of office, and the spurns
That patient merit of th' unworthy
    takes,

When he himself might his quietus
        make
With a bare bodkin? Who would fardels
        bear,
To grunt and sweat under a weary life,
But that the dread of something after
        death,

He reached out, his fingers extending. Genie fought the urge to copy his movement, to seek the answers they could never find in this life. She'd found comfort in these words after Jerome had died, and now she found a different solace—an awakening.

The undiscovered country from whose
        bourn
No traveler returns, puzzles the will
And makes us rather bear those ills
        we have
Than fly to others that we know not of?
Thus conscience does make cowards of
        us all,

He lowered his hand to his side. His gaze moved, just slightly, and Genie imagined he glanced at her. Was she a coward for not performing? No, of course not.

And thus the native hue of resolution
Is sicklied o'er with the pale cast of
        thought,
And enterprises of great pitch and
        moment
With this regard their currents turn
        awry,
And lose the name of action.

A moment of silence passed, then he bowed. The ballroom erupted in applause. Genie wanted desperately for him to continue. Alas, he did not. He bowed again, smiling, then took himself from the dais. He helped Cecilia up, then came back to his seat.

"My goodness, that was thrilling, wasn't it?" Cecilia said, clapping her hands together. "Wonderful. And now for a song from Mrs. Fitzwarren!"

Genie registered what her cousin said, but her focus was on Satterfield as he sat down beside her. "That was brilliant," she whispered. "I wish you could continue."

He looked at her askance. "Thank you."

"Could you?" She angled herself toward him. "Continue, I mean."

"Would you take on the role of Ophelia?" he asked with a slight smile.

"I could."

His gaze locked with hers as Mrs. Fitzwarren began to sing a ballad of love and marriage—rather fitting for this party. Genie wondered if Cecilia had asked her to sing that song in particular.

They turned their attention to the dais. Mrs. Fitzwarren had a beautiful voice. But Genie was still lost in Satterfield's riveting performance. He could have enjoyed a career on the stage.

Genie kept stealing glances toward him, each one longer than the last as she drank in his profile. What was happening?

She forced herself to watch Mrs. Fitzwarren as her voice soared. All the while, she was completely aware of Lord Satterfield's proximity. Maybe just one more look…

As Genie peeked in his direction, her breath caught. He was watching her, his dark eyes smoldering. Had he been stealing glances too?

She couldn't look away. If she dropped her hand

to her side, and he did the same, their fingers might touch…

What was she doing? Genie swung her attention back to Mrs. Fitzwarren and clasped her hands together in her lap.

The song ended, and Genie considered leaving. Except she'd have to move past Lord Satterfield, and right now, she didn't trust herself to even speak to him. Doing so might betray her…what?

"That was lovely," he said, drawing Genie to turn her head.

He'd leaned toward her, and now they were very close. Almost unbearably so. But Genie didn't move. "Yes, but I still enjoyed your performance more," she said softly so that no one else could hear.

His eyes gleamed. "You flatter me."

Genie fought to keep the conversation focused on…anything. "How long did it take you to memorize the speech last night in preparation for today?" She kept her voice just above a whisper.

"None." He also spoke in a low tone. "I committed it to memory years ago. Along with a sonnet or four and a few other favorite speeches from Master Shakespeare's plays."

Oh dear, he loved Shakespeare too. "Is *Hamlet* your favorite?"

"It is indeed."

"Mine is *Much Ado About Nothing*. I adore Beatrice and Benedick."

His lips curled into a brief smile. "A miracle! Here's our own hands against our hearts." He lifted his hand to his chest. "Come, I will have thee, but, by this light, I take thee for pity."

The answering words came to Genie's mind without effort. "I would not deny you, but by this good day, I yield upon great persuasion, and partly to

save your life, for I was told you were in a con-
sumption."

"Peace! I will stop your mouth." His gaze settled
on her lips.

She leaned slightly toward him before realizing
where they were, that Cecilia was back on the dais
announcing the next performance. Her pulse racing,
Genie moved slowly back.

Satterfield did the same. "If Lady Cosford decides
to have another performance, we could do that
scene."

Oh, they couldn't. She was saved from responding
by Mr. Emerson attempting to juggle apples. He was
an absolute disaster, and soon everyone was laughing
at his antics as apples rolled from the dais onto the
floor. Genie was grateful for the distraction.

She was also careful to speak with the person on
her right during the next interlude between performances. Mrs. Sheldon was perhaps a decade or so
younger than Genie. With dark sable hair and
piercing green eyes, she was a beauty.

"You and Lord Satterfield seem to be getting on
well," Mrs. Sheldon said with a warm smile.

Genie didn't want rumors to start. "As well as
anyone. Will you be performing today?"

"Yes. I'll be reciting a poem."

"How wonderful."

"And you?" Mrs. Sheldon asked.

"No." Further conversation was avoided as Cecilia
introduced Mrs. Hatcliff-Lind, who would play the
pianoforte.

Genie slid a glance toward Lord Satterfield, who
gave her a knowing half smile as the first notes were
struck. He mouthed, *See, it's fine.*

She couldn't help but grin and nearly giggled
along with it. Oh, she liked him. And if she wasn't

careful, everyone would notice—if they hadn't already. She wasn't ready to be matched.

Except she could hear Jerome's voice in her head: *Promise me you'll marry again, Genie. I can't bear to think of you alone for so long.*

She'd answered, *Perhaps I'll die tomorrow and you'll recover. Then it's you who must wed.*

He'd laughed, then coughed, and she'd apologized for causing him distress. He'd waved her concern away and taken her hand. *If I were to recover—and if you were taken from me—I would try to find happiness again. It wouldn't be the same. Nothing could ever be. But I would try. I sincerely want you to do the same. Because we both know I'm not going to recover.*

Though two years had passed, and Genie had shed more tears than she could ever count, the memory still pulled at her chest. The sting was less, tempered with a bittersweet joy to have had what they'd shared, even if it had been abbreviated.

No, nothing could ever be the same, nor did Genie want it to be. Still, she had ended up promising him she would try.

Stealing another quick look at Lord Satterfield, Genie wondered if she was ready. She honestly didn't know, and furthermore, didn't know how she *would* know. Perhaps that was her answer.

As soon as the performances ended, Genie hastened to her chamber, where she stayed closeted with her uncertainties until dinner.

CHAPTER 4

*E*dmund took breakfast in his room the following day. He'd stayed up rather late the night before, carousing with a few of the other gentlemen. That wasn't how he'd envisioned his night, but when the dowager duchess had been absent from the drawing room after dinner, Edmund had altered his plans. Disappointed, he'd found consolation in brandy and cards.

She'd also been absent most of yesterday, notably after the performances in the ballroom. Edmund couldn't recall the last time he'd felt so aroused, and not just physically—all from simply sitting beside her.

Well, not just sitting beside her. They'd also talked and traded Shakespearean quotes, and Edmund was nearly completely smitten. Nearly?

There was definitely an attraction, and it seemed mutual. Was it? Was he the reason she'd taken to hiding away in her chamber? He hoped not. And yet he couldn't ignore the thrill that shot through him to think that he was affecting her as keenly as she was affecting him.

He wanted to know for sure. But that was deuced difficult when she didn't come downstairs.

What if she wasn't interested in him? Or if she just wasn't ready for romance again? Perhaps they were doomed when it came to forming a romantic attachment. Since Edmund had come to this party with the intention of finding a potential wife, he ought to consider other women.

Taking a deep breath of resignation, he made his way into the ballroom, where they were to play blind man's buff this afternoon. Several guests were already present, gathered together in a few clusters of conversation. Unfortunately, Edmund didn't see the dowager duchess among them.

Edmund walked toward the nearest group and was immediately intercepted by Lady Bradford as she stepped away from the others. Perhaps five years younger than Edmund, the dowager countess was a stunning blonde of petite height with incandescent pale blue eyes.

"Good afternoon, Lord Satterfield," she said. "Are you ready for blind man's buff?"

"I am. I haven't played in years."

"I have, but with my daughters." She had three girls, and that was all Edmund knew of them.

"How old are they?" he asked.

"Twelve, ten, and seven. Let me just tell you, there is a vast divide between twelve and seven that far exceeds five years," she said with humor. "It is nice to be away for a respite, to be honest."

"I'm sure." He could only imagine, of course.

Another guest joined them. Mrs. Makepeace was the youngest person at the party. At just twenty-five, she'd been married only a little over a year before losing her husband. She was taller than Lady Bradford with a slender frame and dark honey-blonde hair. "I just heard that this version of blind man's buff is to include *kissing*." She waggled her brows.

Lady Bradford grinned. "How lovely. Can you imagine that happening at any other house party?"

Mrs. Makepeace narrowed her eyes playfully. "You'd be surprised at what some people get away with."

"Probably. It's been some time since I attended a house party," Lady Bradford said. "And certainly never one like this."

"It's rather brilliant, though, isn't it?" Mrs. Makepeace looked around the room with glee. "It just feels more…relaxed."

Lady Bradford nodded. "Indeed. The expectations are clear. I feel as though I can be entirely myself."

Edmund couldn't disagree. He also couldn't help but think it was different for him because he was a man. He never felt as if he couldn't be precisely who he wanted to be. "I'm glad you're both enjoying it."

They both swung their heads toward him, but it was Mrs. Makepeace who asked, "Are you? Enjoying the party, that is."

At that moment, the dowager duchess walked into the ballroom. Edmund's pulse picked up. "Immensely."

He found it difficult to resist the urge to walk over and greet her. Instead, he feasted on her elegant gait as she moved into the ballroom. Mr. Sterling met her with a smile, and Edmund watched with blistering annoyance. No, not just annoyance—jealousy.

Lady Bradford and Mrs. Makepeace continued to speak, but Edmund only half listened. They were discussing how kissing might be inserted into blind man's buff. Edmund was only interested insofar as he might get a chance to kiss the dowager duchess.

Eugenia.

Lady Cosford was back on the dais they'd used for their performances the day before. "I think everyone is here. If I have my counting right." She laughed gaily. "As you know, we're going to play blind man's buff. Does anyone *not* know how to play?"

Everyone glanced about, but no one indicated in the affirmative. Edmund couldn't help but shift his gaze to Eugenia. He was pleased to see she was doing the same with him. He smiled at her, but she only half smiled in return. He found that concerning.

"Excellent," Lady Cosford said. "We're going to add a little something to our game today. When the blind man finds and correctly identifies a person, they will kiss them."

There were many verbal responses as well as a few barks of laughter.

"What if I pick Lord Audlington?" Sir Godwin asked.

Lady Cosford pivoted toward Sir Godwin. "You may kiss him however you like—there are no rules as to the type of kiss." She gave him a saucy smile.

Sir Godwin cocked his head. "How about as soon as I realize I've found a gentleman, I purposely lose so I can try again?" More of the guests laughed.

"That is entirely your prerogative," Lady Cosford said. "You may also choose to watch instead of play."

"I'll be watching," Eugenia said. And with that, Edmund's hopes were completely dashed.

Mr. Sterling nodded beside her. "I will too." Then he escorted Lady Kendal to a grouping of chairs nearby.

Edmund stared at them as they sat, close together, their heads bent toward each other. He wanted to sit out too. But before he could get his words past the jealousy burning through him, Lady Cosford announced it was time to start, and she would choose the first name.

After reaching into a bowl, she withdrew a small

piece of parchment and unfolded it. "Lord Satterfield!"

Damn. Now he was stuck.

Lord Cosford came toward him with the blindfold. Edmund had to bend his knees so his host could tie the fabric around his eyes. The last thing he saw before everything went black was Eugenia, her hands folded atop her lap, her head turned toward Sterling, a smile lifting her mouth.

What would happen if Edmund managed to choose her anyway? He silently prayed he'd be able to find a way to see so he could make his way to her chair.

"All right, then?" Cosford asked.

Edmund straightened. He couldn't see a bloody thing. "Yes." The word sounded terse, even to his own ears.

Cosford put his hands on Edmund's biceps and began to turn him about. "Goodness, Satterfield, what sort of exercise are you doing? Your arms are quite muscular!" He laughed as if Edmund's fitness were some sort of jest.

"You only say that because you're skinny as a pole!" someone called. This was met with great laughter.

As Edmund spun about, his equilibrium began to tilt. By the time he stopped, he had no notion of which direction led to Eugenia. He muttered a curse.

"What's that?" Cosford asked.

"I'm bloody dizzy," Edmund said, feeling grouchy. He wanted to get this over with. Then he could decide to sit out and insert himself between Eugenia and Sterling.

"As you should be!"

Edmund didn't recognize who yelled that, nor the laughter that followed. His shoulders were bunched with tension. He forced himself to take a breath and loosen his muscles.

Relax, Edmund. Enjoy yourself. You're here to perhaps find a wife. It doesn't have to be Eugenia. You didn't even know she'd be here.

While that was true, he couldn't help the fact that now he did. And every other woman in attendance was lacking in comparison.

When the floor felt stable beneath Edmund's feet once more, he began to move. Putting his arms out, he felt his way. A quick giggle said he'd come close to a lady. He pivoted and took two large steps. His fingers closed on fabric.

"I have you!" He moved closer and splayed his hand against whomever he'd encountered. He was certain he touched a sleeve. Gliding his palm down, he felt the edge and then flesh. Yes, it was a woman.

He tried to think of who had a gown like that. Better still, he tried to think of the woman's height and who it could match. Pity he hadn't found Lady Bradford—her shorter stature would have given her away for certain.

Edging closer, Edmund moved his hand up the woman's sleeve to her shoulder to determine if this was her back or front. Wrapping his fingers around her collarbone, he slid his hand up to her neck. His fingertips grazed hair at the back—her nape, then. He was facing her. What about her could tell him her identity? He really didn't want to do this more than once. And how did he plan to kiss her?

Hell, all he wanted to do was kiss Eugenia. And not in a ballroom in front of other people. He wanted her alone, preferably in a bedchamber and preferably nude. As his cock twitched, he silently lectured himself to stop thinking of her.

Moving his hand to the front of the mystery woman, he found a brooch pinned to where her fichu met the neckline of her gown. He smiled, for he'd just seen who had been wearing that. "Mrs. Makepeace."

"Remarkable!" a male voice said from nearby.

"I'm correct, then?" Edmund lifted his hand to remove the blindfold.

"Indeed you are, my lord," Mrs. Makepeace said.

Edmund untied the fabric at the back of his head and lowered the blindfold. Mrs. Makepeace gazed up at him, her lips parted. "What sort of kiss will you claim?" she asked, a gleam of flirtation in her hazel eyes.

"What sort do you offer?"

She took a small step so that they nearly touched. "Whatever pleases you."

Edmund looked past her toward where Eugenia sat. Her eyes were locked on Edmund. Her hands were still clasped, but more tightly than before.

Almost without thinking, Edmund lowered his mouth to Mrs. Makepeace's and touched his lips to hers. He didn't stop looking at Eugenia, and so he caught the slight widening of her eyes and the faint blush that rose in her cheeks. Her lips parted, and Edmund wondered if her heart was beating as fast as his. How he wished the mouth he'd just kissed were hers.

He straightened, and the dowager looked away. She lifted her hand to her throat, splaying her fingers just above the hollow as she visibly swallowed.

"That was lovely," Mrs. Makepeace whispered.

"Yes, thank you," Edmund responded. "Now, I believe it's your turn."

"Perhaps I'll find you," she murmured, her eyes glinting coquettishly.

"That would hardly be fair," he said with a chuckle. "I'm going to sit this round out." He found he was in desperate need of a drink. Thankfully, there were refreshments on a table near the dais.

"First, let me tie the blindfold on you." Edmund held up the fabric, and she turned around. He made quick work of securing it around her head. "How's that?"

"I can't see a thing," she said. "Do be careful when you spin me. I am sometimes clumsy."

"I shall do my best." Edmund spun her more sedately than Cosford had done to him, then he took himself to the refreshment table.

Almost immediately, Mrs. Makepeace found Mrs. Sheldon. "I can tell this is a woman," Mrs. Makepeace said. "Can I just keep looking, please?"

Laughter answered her question, then Lady Cosford said, "Yes, go ahead. Perhaps we should have the women move aside for now?"

"What if I want to kiss Mrs. Makepeace?" Lady Clinton asked.

"I say we let her," Mr. Emerson said with a grin.

Edmund shook his head and poured a glass of brandy. He wanted to go and sit next to Eugenia, but he didn't. She didn't look in his direction, not even for a moment. Was she angry that he'd participated in the silly game? She'd had some sort of reaction when she'd watched him kiss Makepeace. Maybe he shouldn't have done it.

Except he was here to perhaps find a wife. And kissing Mrs. Makepeace was part of the exercise. Or he'd done it to provoke Eugenia.

Had it worked? He was damn sure going to find out.

CHAPTER 5

ollowing the ridiculous kissing blind man's buff, the guests went a variety of directions. Some went to play billiards, while others played cards in the drawing room. Still others retired to their rooms—and Genie speculated that Lord Audlington and Mrs. Sheldon were not going upstairs for the purposes of finding rest. Their kiss during the game had gone on a trifle longer than was probably acceptable.

Probably? Nothing about the game had been proper.

Genie regretted not participating.

Only because the moment Lord Satterfield's lips had touched Mrs. Makepeace's, Genie had wanted to scratch the other woman's eyes out. Then she wanted to push her to the floor and take her place.

Her reaction had been swift, violent, and wholly unsettling. She asked herself again, what was happening to her?

After stalking to the library, Genie found a book to read and took it to a small sitting room tucked into the corner of the ground floor far from the billiards and drawing rooms. She considered going up to her chamber, but Mrs. Sheldon's room was next to

hers, and Genie didn't want to hear if she was having
a rendezvous with Lord Audlington.

The sitting room was cozy, with a view of the
damp grounds littered with red and gold leaves being
tossed about by the wind. The rain had stopped—at
least for now—and a few beams of sunlight streaked
through the gray clouds.

She situated herself on a chaise, stretching her
legs out on the cushion and crossing her ankles.
Opening the book, she proceeded to stare at the first
page and not read. She couldn't stop thinking of Satterfield. Of his sensual lips, his piercing gaze, his
muscular arms... Were they in fact muscular? She
longed to find out for herself.

Mrs. Makepeace would know how his lips had
felt. Watching him kiss her had stirred emotions
Genie hadn't felt in some time, or maybe ever.

Oh bother! Unlike everyone else at this party, she
did not come here to find a husband, nor did she
come to have an assignation. She certainly didn't
want to pursue either of those things with Lord Satterfield. She wasn't ready.

Tell that to your body.

Satterfield was obviously angling for a liaison, at
least. He'd been all too eager to participate in the
stupid kissing game and to kiss Mrs. Makepeace on
the mouth. He could just as easily have kissed her
cheek. Better still, her hand.

Scowling, Genie tried to focus on the page in
her lap.

"Good book?"

She snapped the cover closed and leapt to her
feet. It was *him*.

"Did you follow me?"

He sauntered into the sitting room, making the
room feel even smaller than it had a few minutes before. "No."

"Then what are you doing here?"

"Looking for a moment's peace," he said amenably.

"Well, you shan't find it here."

He arched a brow. "Is that right?"

She hadn't meant that to sound argumentative, but now that she'd all but implied it, she squared her shoulders and didn't refute him.

"Should I go?" he asked.

Yes. No. "We can share the room, certainly."

He took another step toward her, leaving just a few feet between them. "You seem angry."

"I'm not." Except her face felt hot, and her body was aquiver. Why was she cross with him?

One more step brought him even closer. And provoked the sensations in her body to a more feverish pitch. "Why didn't you play blind man's buff?"

"I—" She didn't really have a good answer. "I didn't want to kiss anyone." That wasn't precisely true. She didn't want to kiss anyone but him. Oh God, she wanted to kiss him?

He took the final step that put him directly in front of her. She could lift her hands and determine the size of his biceps for herself.

"That's a pity," he said softly. "I was devastated when you sat out."

Devastated? Genie's lips parted as she fought to draw enough breath to support her racing pulse.

"And then you sat down with Sterling, and I'm afraid I was rather jealous. That provoked me to behave in a childish manner. Is it too much for me to hope you were jealous too?"

No, because she was. "I told you I wasn't angry."

His eyes widened, and his nostrils flared slightly. Reveling in catching him off guard, Genie felt emboldened. Standing on her toes, she brought her hand up and curled it around his neck, drawing his head down. Then she touched her lips to his.

With a soft groan, he wrapped his arms around her. She dropped the book to the floor and put her other hand on his bicep. Squeezing, she satisfied her curiosity as best as she could given the layers of his clothing. Oh yes, he was quite well formed.

And his lips were divine. She'd almost forgotten how delightful a simple kiss could be, the way her body quickened and the flames of arousal began to flicker.

He clasped her back and brought her flush against him. Angling his head, he licked his tongue along her lips. Genie opened for him, inviting his entry, sliding her tongue along his in a merry chase.

Wild sensation careened through her. This seemed at once forbidden and desperately necessary. She shouldn't want this. She couldn't want this…not yet?

She pulled her mouth from his and lowered her feet. Her breath came hard and fast. "I—it's too soon."

"Is it?" He didn't let her go. "Why?"

"Because…" She had no answer. Again, she heard Jerome's voice telling her to be happy. He would want her to do this. Still, she was conflicted. "It feels strange."

He took his hands from her. "I'm sorry to hear that. I think it feels rather wonderful."

She saw the flash of disappointment in his gaze, the struggle within him not to show her his hurt. "It's not you," she rushed to say. "I'm…drawn to you. I *was* jealous of you kissing Mrs. Makepeace."

"Would it help to know I was thinking of kissing you?"

"Yes." She ought to have been ashamed to admit it, but she was smiling instead.

He took her hand. "Duchess." He looked her in the eye. "Eugenia."

She ran her thumb along his hand. "Genie."

"Genie." He said her name like a vocal caress, evoking a shiver along her shoulders. "I will go as slowly as you like. I am not interested in Mrs. Makepeace or anyone else."

Joy sparked inside her. She glanced down at their joined hands. Then she looked back up at him and put her palm against his cheek. "I didn't come here to make a match. Or to have a liaison."

"I did. To *perhaps* make a match," he clarified. "It's probably time I take a wife, or so my mother has been telling me for the past decade." He cracked a smile.

"I don't know if I'm ready for that." She ran her thumb along his supple lower lip. "I am, however, ready for another kiss. Are you?"

"More than."

She rose on her toes again as he swept her against him. His mouth crashed against hers. She plunged her fingers into his hair, cupping his head as she held on to him fiercely. His hands moved across her upper back and then lower, one of them clutching her backside.

She pressed into him, her sex pulsing with need. Perhaps a liaison would be welcome…

By the time they separated, they were both breathing hard. He rested his forehead against hers. "I didn't close the door."

"Oh." She should be scandalized, but she couldn't muster even a modicum of horror or regret. She clutched his lapels and brushed her lips against his once more. "I'm going upstairs to get ready for dinner. Please don't follow me. This is…lovely. It's also more than I anticipated."

He nodded once. "I understand. I'm a patient man, Genie."

She looked up at him. "I'm not making any promises."

"And I have no expectations." He smiled broadly. "Just all the hope in the world."

~

*A*fter dinner that night, the women adjourned to the drawing room as usual. Genie took a chair situated with a small settee and another pair of chairs. Lady Bradford, Mrs. Grey, and Lady Clinton joined her as the other ladies gathered together near the fireplace.

Genie knew Lady Bradford—Lettie—quite well and was somewhat acquainted with Mrs. Grey. She'd met Lady Clinton only a few times. Lady Clinton and Mrs. Grey sat together on the settee, while Lettie sat in a chair angled next to Genie's.

Lady Clinton, who was several years younger than Genie with dark red hair and wide brown eyes, glanced around at everyone in their circle. "Lady Cosford has done such a wonderful job with this party. I can't believe it's almost half over. Do you think there is any chance she can make it last longer?"

"You're missing your children as much as I am?" Mrs. Grey asked sardonically. She was perhaps even younger than Lady Clinton, which made Genie realize she might very well be one of the oldest guests, if not *the* oldest. They both laughed, and Lettie joined in.

Genie smiled but couldn't bring herself to laugh with the others. She had no children of her own, not anymore. She had her stepson, Titus, of course, but he was well past the age of depending on her. Her daughter, Eliza, would be sixteen if she'd lived. Sometimes, Genie thought about the things they would be doing.

"My apologies, Genie," Lettie said warmly. She knew Genie had lost Eliza to illness at the age of three.

"It's all right. It is a nice party." *Nice.* That word didn't adequately describe Lord Satterfield's kiss. Was she really going to continue to think of him as "Lord Satterfield" now? Did he go by Edmund or some other name?

Mrs. Grey turned toward Genie, her blue eyes inquisitive. "Your Grace, why didn't you play blind man's buff earlier?"

Genie considered telling her a fib—that she didn't like to be blindfolded or she hated feeling dizzy. But instead, she was honest. "I'm not quite ready for a match."

"Kissing isn't a match, especially at this party," Lady Clinton said, adjusting her necklace so the amber cross rested just below the hollow of her throat. "Especially if it's up to Sir Nathaniel to do the kissing." She rolled her eyes as she referred to the way he'd kissed her upon finding and correctly guessing her identity. He'd pressed a chaste kiss to the back of her hand.

Everyone laughed, and Mrs. Grey said in a whisper, "It could have been far worse. Mr. Howell could have tried to shove his tongue down your throat."

"I wondered if that's what he was trying," Lettie said, shaking her head.

"I accidentally stepped on his foot. *Hard.*" Mrs. Grey smiled demurely. "Thankfully, he was wearing slippers instead of boots."

"I do understand your reticence," Lady Clinton said. "I'm in no hurry to wed either. Twice may be quite enough."

Genie had forgotten that the viscountess had been married twice. "Would you consider it a third time?" She wasn't sure she could risk it. The thought of losing another husband filled her with dread.

"Honestly, I don't know." Lady Clinton dropped her voice. "My second marriage wasn't a love match. My boys needed a father, his daughter needed a mother." She shrugged. "It was good enough, and he did give me my third son, whom I adore." Her eyes lit with joy. "But I wouldn't do that again, not after knowing how much better it is to be in love with your husband."

Mrs. Grey brushed at one of the light brown curls against her temple. "You loved your first husband, then?"

"More than anything," Lady Clinton said softly, her lips curling into a faint smile. "If I could have that again, I'd do it a third—and a fourth—time. But I don't know if anyone can be that fortunate. Once is astonishing. Twice is...nearly impossible."

Genie's chest constricted. She felt precisely the same way. She'd loved Jerome so much. And he'd loved her. His experience had been the reverse of Lady Clinton. His first marriage had been arranged and bereft of affection. When he'd married again, he'd made certain he loved his bride.

"I know what you mean," Genie said, giving her a look of support. "I'm not sure it's possible either."

"Well, I would just like to fall in love," Lettie said with a laugh. "I cared for my husband, but there was no grand emotion." She turned to Mrs. Grey. "What about you?"

"I did love him." Mrs. Grey's voice was quiet. "I don't think he felt the same. At least not for me. His mistress may have had a different experience."

Lady Clinton reached over and clasped Mrs. Grey's hand. "Men can be awful. My husband had a

mistress too, but I didn't care. In fact, I'd been contemplating my own liaison before he died." She gave
them all a sly smile, and it lightened the mood once
more.

Except Genie still felt as if she'd swallowed lead.
She didn't want to mislead Edmund.

She stood abruptly. "Please excuse me, I'm going
to retire for the evening. See you all tomorrow." She
smiled then went to bid a quick good-night to her
cousin before hastening from the drawing room. She
didn't want to be there when the men arrived.

As she made her way to her chamber, the kisses
she and Edmund had shared earlier were at the fore-
front of her mind. She'd thought of little else since
that afternoon. At dinner, they'd been seated on the
same side of the table, though a few chairs apart, so
she hadn't been able to see him. That was probably
for the best, as she didn't think she could have kept
herself from looking at him all evening.

She forced herself to consider whether she would
marry again. Maybe? Especially if there were children for her to mother. Edmund didn't have any because he'd never been married.

Why was she thinking of marriage to him? He
hadn't mentioned it. He'd only indicated that he
wanted to kiss her again. Perhaps he was only interested in a liaison while they were here.

Would that be…bad?

Genie didn't have an answer. Hopefully, tomorrow she would. As Lady Clinton had said, the
party was almost half over.

She was running out of time.

CHAPTER 6

*W*hen Edmund arrived in the drawing room after dinner the night before and found that Genie had already retired, he worried he'd ruined things. Except, she'd initiated that first kiss and had been a willing participant in the others.

Thankfully, he'd seen her at breakfast, and she'd been her usual charming self. No, not usual. She'd been a touch enigmatic. Or, perhaps it was that Edmund was looking for behavior and attitude that didn't exist. Because he wanted to see his longing—his desire—reflected back.

They'd played parlor games earlier and were now going to set off for a walk to the River Swift since the weather had dried. As they gathered just behind the house, the guests collected in groups. A couple of pairings seemed somewhat certain. Mrs. Fitzwarren and Sir Godwin, as well as Mrs. Sheldon and Lord Audlington, appeared to have formed attachments. Whether they would be permanent remained to be seen.

Edmund kept his eye on the door, waiting for Genie to appear. He was so focused that he failed to see Mrs. Makepeace approach him. "I'm so pleased the weather cleared so we could get outside," she said.

"Indeed." He gave her a smile while still trying to keep his attention somewhat on the door.

"I'm looking forward to the dancing competition later. Just when I think Lady Cosford can't possibly come up with a new activity, she does."

At last, Genie came outside. However, she was immediately followed by Sterling, and it was clear they'd met up inside and walked out together. *Blast.*

"Are we all ready?" Cosford called out from beside his wife. "On the way, we'll stop at the new folly. It's not finished, but it's well underway. Then we'll continue to the river, where we'll have refreshments. Don't get lost now!" He grinned, then pivoted to present his arm to Lady Cosford. They led the procession.

Edmund didn't see how he could possibly escort Genie as he'd hoped. Resigned, he offered Mrs. Makepeace his arm.

"Thank you," she said, curling her hand around his sleeve. They started through the garden, which had been designed by Capability Brown fifty years earlier. "I would love to have seen this garden in the summer."

"I have—not this year—and it's stunning," Edmund said as they walked through the rose garden.

They walked in silence for a minute or so before she asked, "Are you enjoying the party?"

"Yes, you?"

"More than I anticipated, actually."

"Why is that?"

"I worried I would be the youngest person here." Mrs. Makepeace smiled. "I suppose I am, but I don't feel as if I don't belong. Everyone's been married before." She glanced at him. "Not quite everyone. The women I mean. You are unwed, are you not?"

"I have not married, no."

"And are you here because you wish to change that, or…" She let the rest of her question hang in the air.

Or was he here for an assignation? Or perhaps more than one assignation. He didn't think anyone here would try that, but he had his suspicions about Howell. Edmund chose his words carefully. "I've never been opposed to marriage. I just haven't met the right woman yet."

"That's admirable you're waiting for a love match. I hope you find it."

Edmund suspected he already had.

He turned the conversation to the colors of autumn, and they soon arrived at the folly. Designed to look like a ruined Grecian temple, the structure was maybe half finished.

"Will you have a hermit?" Lord Pritchard asked loudly. "If so, perhaps young Dryden here will apply for the position."

Dryden was the youngest gentleman in attendance. Slightly shy, he'd recently inherited a fortune. He'd come here in the hope that he'd avoid the Marriage Mart next Season when he would almost certainly be overwhelmed with attention.

"How much are you paying?" Dryden called toward Cosford.

"For you? Nothing!" Cosford returned with a laugh. "You can pay me!"

This was met with guffaws and laughter.

Lady Bradford and Mr. Emerson joined Edmund and Mrs. Makepeace. "I was just telling Mr. Emerson that all of you unmarried gentlemen should apply to be Cosford's hermit," Lady Bradford said with a laugh.

Emerson shook his head with a chuckle. "And I

explained that just because we aren't wed doesn't mean we wish to live alone in a faux ruin."

"Precisely," Edmund agreed. "Where would be the fun in that?" He scanned the gathering and found Genie standing closer to the folly. She was still with Sterling, dammit.

"I wonder if they're pairing off," Lady Bradford said, moving close to Edmund as Emerson spoke with Mrs. Makepeace.

Edmund wasn't certain the countess had seen where he was looking. He would pretend she hadn't. "Whom are you speaking of?"

"The dowager duchess and Mr. Sterling. Weren't you looking at them?" She paused only briefly before continuing—thankfully, so that he didn't have to actually answer the question. "Seems as though some are doing that, which makes sense as we are at the halfway point of the party."

"Lady Cosford should feel very accomplished," Edmund said.

"Honestly, this is a brilliant idea for a party—no simpering misses with their overbearing mothers." Lady Bradford laughed. "I should be careful. I may be one of those overbearing mothers in the not so distant future."

Lord and Lady Cosford started toward the river once more, and Edmund again presented his arm to a woman who wasn't Genie. He kept up a conversation with Lady Bradford despite Genie occupying a large piece of his mind. If the purpose of this party was to meet someone you wanted to spend time with— whether temporarily or permanently—Edmund was already there.

But was Genie? She'd retired early last night, and so far today, he'd had no opportunity to speak with her. Did she regret kissing him? He hoped not. Those kisses had been everything he'd dreamed and more.

At the river, a table had been set up with an array of food and drink. Edmund didn't care about any of it. His primary focus was getting to Genie and making sure she walked back to the house on *his* arm.

He managed to take care not to walk directly to her. Chatting with people as he went, he made his way toward her. Annoyingly, Sterling was *still* at her side.

But unannoyingly, her eyes sparked with pleasure the moment she saw Edmund. He couldn't help smiling in response.

"Good afternoon, Lord Satterfield," she said.

"Good afternoon, Duchess." He glanced toward Sterling to acknowledge him. "Sterling. I believe Lady Bradford was hoping to have a word with you." Edmund didn't know where that lie had come from and didn't care.

Sterling turned to Genie and took her hand. "Thank you for the lovely company. I hope to see you later." He pressed a kiss to the back of her hand, then nodded toward Edmund before taking himself off.

Edmund hoped he would walk straight into the river.

"You're glaring at him," Genie whispered.

Blinking, Edmund moved his attention to her. "Was I?"

Genie's mouth tipped into a sly smile. "I think you know you were. Did Lady Bradford really want to talk to him?"

"Probably?" Edmund lifted a shoulder as he stepped closer to her. "I'm sure she will by the time he arrives." He was relieved to see Genie wasn't upset with him for sending Sterling away. In fact, she seemed to be flirting. "You don't mind that he left?"

She shook her head. "How was your walk with Lady Bradford and Mrs. Makepeace?"

"Tolerable."

Genie's shoulders twitched.

"How was yours with Sterling?"

"Also tolerable." She inhaled. "No, that isn't fair. It was nice actually. He's quite charming. He spoke of his children."

"Mrs. Makepeace and Lady Bradford both speculated about the matches that may or may not be going on. Lady Bradford suggested you and Sterling were perhaps pairing off." He didn't ask the question, but held his breath, hoping she would refute it.

"I'm not pairing off with anyone," she said, which was both a good and bad answer.

"I was rather hoping you might be." He looked into her eyes, his voice soft.

She cocked her head slightly so that her mouth was nearer his ear. To anyone glancing in their direction, they would likely appear to be having an intimate conversation. But then, they were.

"Just because I may be interested in a small...indulgence this week, doesn't mean I'm part of a pair."

His heart began to race. Was she saying...? "If it matters to you, I am most interested in an indulgence." Her eyes widened almost imperceptibly, and he wanted to be explicit. "With you. And only you."

"I see." Her tongue peeked out and wetted her lips. Edmund went completely hard and shifted his body toward the river.

"Aren't you going to come have refreshments?" Lady Cosford asked as she approached. "Come, there's a special ale that Cosford had the brewer make." She smiled brightly, and they had no choice but to go with her. To do otherwise would have been rude.

Except that Edmund had a troublesome erection to deal with. "I'll be there shortly. I just want to take in the river for a moment."

"It's a beautiful vista," Genie said. "We were just

discussing that." Definitely not how they both wanted to have an affair. That was what she'd meant, wasn't it? God, he hoped so.

Lady Cosford nodded. "We do love to spend time here. Did I mention there are lavender cakes? I know how much you like those, Genie."

"I do indeed." She looped her arm through her cousin's and gave Edmund a long look before departing.

Edmund exhaled as his body finally began to listen to the urgings of his mind. Later, there would be ample opportunity to let himself go. He hoped.

He was almost completely certain that was what Genie had meant—that she wanted to conduct a liaison. But was that all? He wanted more.

Patience.

Yes, patience. He'd waited this long, and she was well worth it.

~

When the clock in Genie's room struck one, she finally deemed it late enough to leave. As she stepped from her chamber, she hesitated. What if he wasn't in his room yet? How late did the gentlemen stay up?

She should have planned this with him!

Except, she hadn't wanted to commit. She'd been too afraid she'd change her mind. Even now, she was vacillating.

Just go. You want this. And there's nothing wrong with wanting it. Wanting him.

Inhaling sharply, she recalled the path to Edmund's room. She'd stared at the map so much, it would have been impossible for her to forget where his chamber was located. Thankfully, he was on the same side of the house. She just hoped she didn't encounter anyone on the way.

Because of that, she walked quickly and found herself at his door far sooner than she'd anticipated. Again, she hesitated.

You've come this far. Don't stop now!

She lifted her hand to knock on the door. What if his valet answered?

Freezing in horror, she almost turned. But the insistent throb between her legs kept her still. All during dinner and the outrageously entertaining dance competition, she'd watched him—and he'd watched her. It had seemed there was an unspoken communication, a mutual desire swelling between them.

What if she was wrong?

Knock. On. The. Door.

Genie rapped her knuckles briskly against the wood before she could talk herself out of it. Then she squeezed her eyes shut and prayed it was him—and only him—who answered the door. Oh God, what if he had another *guest*?

She began to pivot just as the door opened. Whipping her head toward the room, she saw that it was, in fact, just Edmund.

Surprise flashed in his gaze, and he opened the door wider. "Thank goodness it's you. Come in."

She didn't move right away. He took her hand and gently tugged her inside, then closed the door behind her.

He gave her an apologetic smile. "I don't think you want to be seen standing out there. In case anyone happens by."

"No, I wouldn't. Thank you. I'm sorry. I'm... I don't know what to say. Or do. Or...anything."

"Let's start with good evening, shall we?" He

squeezed her hand. "Good evening, Genie. I'm so pleased to see you. Surprised, but pleased."

"Are you really? Surprised, I mean. I thought..." She exhaled. "I don't know what I thought. My thoughts change with every moment."

He took her other hand and looked into her eyes. "Why don't we just sit and talk. Would you like brandy? Port? Madeira?"

"You have all those things here?"

"No, but I could get them."

"That won't be necessary. I'll have whatever is convenient."

He nodded once. "Would you like to sit by the hearth?" He gestured to where a small settee was situated in front of the low-burning fire.

"Yes, thank you." Genie went to sit down, her legs wobbling nervously. She turned her head to see where he'd gone to pour the drinks. The bed, standing against the wall opposite the hearth, loomed large and intimidating.

This was a mistake.

No, it isn't. Sit down!

Genie lowered herself to the settee and told herself she was being utterly foolish. She was as agitated as a new bride. Thinking back to her wedding night, she tried to recall if she'd been this nervous. No, she hadn't.

Then why was she now? Was it because they weren't married? Or perhaps this wasn't nervousness but anticipation.

Edmund appeared in front of her. "Here. It's brandy." He handed her a glass, and she registered what she hadn't in the fog of her discomposure. He wore his breeches and shirt, which was open and revealed dark hair on his chest—possibly more hair than was on top of his head, which she found absurdly amusing, likely due to her current state of apparent lunacy.

He sat down beside her on the settee and sipped his brandy. "To answer your query, yes, I am truly surprised to see you here."

Genie took a drink to fortify her nerves—if that was even possible. "You made it clear you are interested in a liaison. I am not...uninterested."

He laughed softly. "I might have hoped for more enthusiasm."

She blushed. "I am enthusiastic. I am also nervous." She took a longer drink of the brandy. "I thought this was a regular house party. When I learned it was being held to afford widows the opportunity to make a match or just have an assignation, I wanted to leave. But the weather interfered, and I could not. Then I met you." Her gaze connected with his. "I didn't expect..." She didn't know what to say next.

"You didn't expect to be attracted to me?" He sounded hopeful.

"Yes. I didn't expect to be attracted to anyone." She looked toward the fire. "I loved my husband deeply. I miss him terribly, and I expect I always will."

There was silence for a long moment before he asked, "Do you question whether there is a place for anyone else in your future?"

She returned her gaze to his. "Yes. Precisely. I don't expect to find another love."

His smile was sad. "Well, that is rather discouraging—for you and for me."

Oh dear. He'd hoped for...something, apparently. She reached over and put her hand on his.

"Why did you come here tonight?" he asked.

A tremor ran through her. She straightened, pushing her uncertainty aside. If she was honest with herself, she knew what she wanted. "Because since we kissed yesterday, I've thought of little else." She shook her head. "No, it was before that. Watching you perform Shakespeare, I was moved by the depth of your emotion. There is something about you I find compelling. All this morning as I walked to the river with Sterling, I observed you with Mrs. Makepeace and then Lady Bradford. I contemplated how I might push them aside and take their place. Tonight at dinner, I was frustrated that we still weren't seated beside each other. Then in the dancing competition, I was even more annoyed that we weren't ever paired together. So here I am."

His eyes sparked with heat and mirth. "Duchess, I am astonished. And flattered. Most of all, I am encouraged. Here we are, two people who are attracted to—and compelled by, for I feel the same about you— one another. Alone. In a bedchamber. What shall we do about it?" He looked at her in such a provoking fashion—his gaze devouring her as it moved from her face down over her body.

Emboldened, she took his glass and stood, putting it and hers on the mantel. Then she turned to face him and unbuttoned her dressing gown. Surprisingly, her fingers didn't so much as quiver.

Genie removed the garment and draped it over the back of the settee. Then she put her knee on the settee and leaned over him. "Shall I stay?"

His eyes darkened to near pitch. "Yes, please." The words were thick and heavy, resonating in the pit of Genie's belly.

Bracing her hand on the back of the settee, she lowered her head and kissed him, her mouth brushing gently over his. They played a moment, their lips and tongues seeking and teasing, touching and withdrawing.

He brought his hand up and cupped her nape. Pulling her head to his, he brought their lips together and sank his tongue into her mouth, devouring her as he had with his gaze. Sensation pulsed through her. It had been so long since she'd felt this.

His fingers dug into her hair, the bulk of which hung in a braid down her back. She pressed down against him, her breasts crushing against his chest. He dragged his thumb along the edge of her ear as he kissed her, long, deep strokes of his tongue against hers. She put her other hand on his shoulder, clutching him as waves of want crested within her.

The heat of his body seeped through the lawn of his shirt. She moved her hand up and slid it beneath the fabric. The feel of his flesh against hers was beyond enticing. She wanted more, needed more.

He clasped her waist and pushed her back against the other end of the settee, somewhat reversing their positions. Rising over her, he stared down at her with naked lust.

"Genie, I have never wanted another woman as much as I want you. Does that frighten you? It frightens me."

She wasn't scared. Not of him. Not of this. She shook her head and lifted her hand. "Come to me, Edmund."

He reached for the hem of her night rail and pulled it up to her waist. She lifted her hips, and together they rid her of the garment. When she lay before him nude, she couldn't help but wonder if she was enough. She was no longer young.

He let out a sharp hiss. "You are so beautiful. Perfect, in fact."

She let out a shaky laugh. "That can hardly be true."

Riveted on her, he cupped her breast. "It is true. You are perfect to me in every way." He ran his thumb over her nipple, sending a burst of sensation to her sex.

She cast her head back and closed her eyes, giving herself over to his touch. "Yes." She'd never shied from asking for what she wanted or instigating what she desired.

He repeated the action with her other breast—cupping, then tweaking her nipple softly.

She moaned softly. "More."

He pinched her then. She jerked, her body lifting from the settee, and she cried out. His mouth closed around her, and he teased her with lips and tongue before sucking hard. Genie put her hands on his head and held him to her. He cupped her other breast, driving her to a fit of need that pooled between her legs. Her hips moved, of their own volition really, eager for his touch.

He seemed to understand what she wanted for his hand moved down her rib cage and abdomen, his fingers stroking her flesh as he descended to the apex of her thighs. He touched her sex, his hand pressing gently against her mound before his finger glided along her folds. He drew hard on her nipple as he slipped his finger into her. Genie rose up, meeting his thrust and gasping. He lifted his head and kissed her again, taking her whimpers into his mouth as he pumped his finger into her.

She moved, her hips rising with each stroke. Then his mouth was gone from hers. He kissed along her jaw and throat, licking and nipping his way down to her breasts once more, then lower still.

No, he couldn't mean to... Yes, he meant to. He licked her clitoris, then sucked, sending a sharp spear of pleasure straight through her core. She held his head and tried to keep herself from completely falling apart. Not yet.

But he was relentless in his efforts. His mouth and fingers worked in and out of her, rousing her to heights of desire she wasn't sure she recalled. She cried out as sensation overwhelmed her. He licked into her, thrust his tongue deep into her sex, and she tumbled into the dark intensity of her orgasm. Her body shuddered as her muscles clenched. She cried out again and again, unable to find herself as she fell through time and space.

He didn't stop until she emerged from the darkness. Then he swept her into his arms and carried her to the bed. She managed to recover enough to scramble to her knees on the bed. She reached for him, pulling his shirt from his breeches. He lifted his arms so she could pull it over his head.

Now he was exposed to her, she could see he was every bit as muscular as others had said during the party. Dark hair covered the center of his chest and around his nipples. He was the most masculine thing she'd ever seen—or felt. She ran her hands over him, reveling in his hardness and heat. Skimming her palms up his chest, she cupped his neck and pulled his head down so she could kiss him.

She tasted herself on his tongue, which only fueled her desire. How long was this night? Not long enough, she reckoned. Not for all the ways she wanted to explore him and have him study her.

He began to unbutton his fall, but she lowered her hands to finish the task, pushing his aside. When the breeches were loose, she pushed them down his hips. He assisted then—and she allowed it—which meant she could touch him. She wrapped her hand around his shaft. Velvety soft and rock hard, she stroked him from balls to tip. The urge to put her mouth around him was strong, but she was too eager to feel him inside her.

She whispered next to his ear, "Shall I lie back? Or shall you? Or shall I get on my knees?"

He groaned in response. "You are beyond imagination. Yes, yes, and yes. I want to sink myself inside you until I don't know where I end and you begin. By morning, I won't remember what it feels like to be without you, nor do I want to."

His words enflamed her. She worked her hand around him, pulling another groan from his throat.

"Genie, look at me." He cupped the back of her head. "What do *you* want?"

"You inside me. Now. I don't care how." She straightened her legs out and sat down on the coverlet, scooting to the edge of the bed so she could put the tip of his cock against her sex.

"Then now you shall have me." He narrowed his eyes and pushed her back onto the bed so she lay flat. Then he moved her farther onto the mattress so that he climbed over her. She closed her eyes as his fingers stroked her folds and clitoris, stoking her desire.

His cock pressed against her. "Look at me, Genie." She opened her eyes. "Look at me as we come together. Tell me this is what you want."

"It is. I want this. I want *you*."

CHAPTER 7

*E*dmund never wanted this moment to end. Since the start of the party, he'd allowed himself to hope that a long-dead dream might actually come to fruition. Now that it was here, he was humbled and overwhelmed. That she, his goddess, was finally here nearly undid him.

He cupped the side of her head as he guided himself into her, sliding deep inside. A deep, sultry sound burst from his throat as he felt her clench around him, welcoming him. If he lived to be a hundred, there would never be another moment like this. Nor did he want there to be. This was everything he'd ever craved and more.

The moment froze in his mind—her dark lashes brushing her cheeks as her eyes closed in ecstasy. Her pink lips parted as a soft moan escaped her mouth. She was the most beautiful thing he'd ever seen. And she was his.

Edmund moved within her, withdrawing and thrusting, slowly and methodically at first, his body learning hers and hers learning his. They fit together perfectly—at least in his mind. She rose to meet him, their bodies meeting in a divine rhythm.

Her legs wrapped right around him, her hands

clasping his lower back. "Yes, yes," she murmured over and over. "Faster, please."

He complied, driving into her with greater speed. He wanted this to last forever, but knew that wasn't possible. "Genie," he murmured, overcome with desire and emotion. He kissed her, their tongues and moans mingling as their bodies moved together.

Suddenly, her muscles clenched, and she cried out. Her feet dug into his backside as her sex squeezed him. His balls tightened, and he barely held back his orgasm.

"Do I need to remove myself?" he managed to ask. He'd meant to settle that question beforehand, but he'd been quite carried away.

"No," she rasped. "Come, Edmund. Come with me."

It was all the urging he needed. He drove into her several more times as his orgasm built. Then he rushed over the edge, shouting her name as he spent himself inside her.

He'd no notion of how much time passed before he moved again. She held him tenderly, her lips brushing against his cheek and lips. He kissed her softly before he withdrew from her body and rolled to his side. When he recaptured his breath, he pulled the coverlet down and tucked her beneath it before joining her.

He gathered her in his arms and kissed her temple. "That was magnificent."

"Yes, it was rather...lovely." She kissed his throat and snuggled into him. "I never expected to have that. Not again."

He knew she'd loved Kendal, even before she'd told him. He also imagined it must be difficult to move on without him. He tried to think of what he might do if he lost her. No, that wasn't the same. They were not wed. They were not in love.

As far as he knew.

He, of course, had nurtured feelings for her long ago. He'd never imagined he might have the opportunity to explore them or that she might love him in return. And he still couldn't quite conceive of it. "I am humbled that you would share this with me."

She pulled back so they faced each other. "How are you not married? You are kind and charming. Intelligent, handsome, extremely accomplished in the physical arts—"

"Physical arts?" He laughed, then kissed her. "That is wonderful."

"What else should I say? You've a talent with your mouth? And other things?" She blushed, then laughed. "I swear, I'm not a prude. It's just been some time, and as I said, I never dreamed I'd be doing this again. Let alone enjoying it so much." She blanched. "Is that bad?"

He kissed her soundly. "No. Surely your husband would have wanted you to continue to live, to find happiness again. I would want that for my wife."

"Jerome did want that. He made me promise, in fact." She looked at him intently. "You didn't answer my question. Why aren't you wed?"

Edmund couldn't quite bring himself to tell her the truth. Because it was a truth he'd never acknowledged, and still hadn't—not entirely. "I've never been moved to. You fell in love with Kendal, did you not?" At her nod, he said, "I haven't been fortunate enough to fall in love with someone and have them do the same."

"I'm sorry." Her forehead creased, and she looked at him with genuine sympathy, but not pity. There was a difference. "You came to the party hoping that might change?"

"I did. As much as my mother nags me about marrying and producing an heir—she's right. I have a duty. Perhaps it's time I look past my romantic necessities and trust that love will come."

"It doesn't always. My eldest sister loathes her husband. They haven't shared a bed in twenty years. He has a long-term mistress, and my sister has recently—finally—embarked on an affair of her own. I'm glad for her, but overall, it's a sad state."

"I suppose that's what I've wanted to avoid. I fear a loveless marriage would be intolerable, duty or no."

She gazed at him with such warmth that his heart swelled. "You do have romantic necessities, don't you?"

He laughed. "My mother calls me hopelessly romantic and sees it as a detriment."

"I disagree. Any woman fortunate enough to fall in love with you will be lucky beyond measure."

Edmund couldn't help but note that she didn't speak like a woman who might be in love. But it was surely too soon for that—at least for her. "That's kind of you to say."

She grimaced. "I'm not helping you find a wife. I'm distracting you. I should not have come tonight."

He cupped her face. "No. You are the only woman at this party I am interested in."

Something—understanding, maybe—flickered in her eyes. "You want an heir?"

"It is my duty," he said simply. He supposed he wanted children—he enjoyed his nieces and nephews. "Perhaps we just made one." He winked at her.

Her eyes widened, and her brows pitched low on her forehead as she pulled back. She sat up abruptly, holding the coverlet to her chest. "That isn't possible. I can't have any more children."

Edmund sat up with her. Any more? She'd had children? He didn't recall, perhaps because he'd purposely not paid attention to her marriage despite being friendly with her husband. "Do you have children? I wasn't aware."

"I had a daughter," she said softly, her gaze focused on the fireplace. "Eliza. She died when she was three."

"Tell me about her."

Genie's eyes lit. "She was bright and funny, so quick to laugh. She loved to follow her older half brother around. Titus was so good with her. He would read her stories, especially after she got sick." Her expression dimmed, and Edmund gently stroked his fingers along her spine. "I lost three more after her—well before their term—and wasn't able to conceive at all the last five years of my marriage. The physician said I was past my childbearing years."

He frowned. "Physicians can be wrong."

She snapped her gaze to his. "I have long given up hope for any more children and would ask that you don't speak of such things. It's not kind."

Anguished by her obvious heartache, he took her hand. "I didn't mean to be unkind."

"I'm forty-two, Edmund," she said quietly. "I cannot give you an heir."

He wished he could say he didn't want one, that he didn't need one. But the fact was that he did have a duty. Troubled, he stroked his thumb over her hand.

She took a deep breath and looked at him. "You should know that losing my daughter was even more painful than losing Jerome. I miss him terribly, but you've shown me there is life after him. My stepson, Titus, showed me that I could be a mother, even if the child wasn't of my blood. If I marry again, I would hope to have the chance to mother my husband's children."

Her words cut into him. She wasn't interested in marriage, at least not to him. To realize his dream and have it dashed all in the same night was a blow he couldn't have foreseen.

Edmund rolled over and got up from the bed. He padded to the armoire and fetched his banyan. Wrapping it around his now-cold body, he tied the sash and turned. She'd also left the bed and had gone to the settee where she drew the night rail over her exquisite form.

She put her feet into the slippers that she'd kicked off at some point, then donned her dressing gown. He wanted to stop her, to ask her to stay. He'd envisioned a night full of learning each other's bodies, giving pleasure, and blissful surrender.

But that was not to be. Not after the revelations of their stark truths.

Still, they had shared a wonderful experience. He went to stand before her as she finished buttoning her dressing gown. Several strands of hair had come free of her plait and curled gently against her cheeks and temples.

He fingered one of those curls and gave her a half smile. "Tonight was remarkable. There are two more nights left. I would count myself lucky if you wanted to share them with me."

She stared at him, her lips parted. "I don't know. This was…exceptional. I will treasure the memory always." She put her palm against his cheek and stood on her toes to kiss him.

Edmund wrapped his arms around her and gathered her close. He claimed her mouth, sliding his tongue against hers, hopefully reminding her of how well they fit together, of how good they were.

When he released her, she gasped for air. Her gaze settled intently on his for a long moment. "Good night, Edmund."

"Good night, Genie."

She turned and he followed her, opening the

door, then closing it after watching her walk away. He nearly went after her and begged her to come back. No, he wanted to beg her to reconsider what she wanted. Was there any way she might want him? Not just for now, but forever?

He couldn't see it, not if she wanted to mother children. He had none, and apparently, she couldn't have any.

It was a very long time before he slept.

~

*a*t breakfast the following morning, Lord Cosford had announced they would ride in the afternoon if the weather continued to remain dry. This had generated a sense of excitement. Now, as most had gathered in the drawing room following breakfast, there was a fraught energy, as if everyone couldn't wait to get out.

Or perhaps that was simply Genie's inner agitation. She'd barely slept after visiting Edmund the night before.

Her gaze found him across the room. She'd keep a surreptitious eye on him all day, and it seemed he'd done the same. Any time their eyes met, she looked away. Did he do the same? And were they going to avoid each other for the rest of the party? Tomorrow would be the last full day, so she supposed it was possible.

It was also probably for the best. Then why did she feel sad?

She went to pluck a biscuit from a plate on a table in the corner. There was never a shortage of food or drink at Blickton.

"Good choice. Those are my favorite." Edmund's voice sent a quiver of delight up her spine.

Genie turned to face him as he picked up one of

the biscuits. "Mine too. But then I like lavender any-thing. And lemon." The biscuit combined both flavors.

Seeing him this close made Genie's chest swell and then abruptly tighten. While she would cherish last night, she couldn't help thinking it would be best if it hadn't happened.

"I wanted to apologize," she said softly.

His dark brows gathered on his wide forehead. "For what?"

"For last night. I should not have come to your room. It was ill conceived of me."

His features relaxed, and one side of his mouth briefly quirked up. "I thought it was rather brilliant," he murmured.

She fought a blush, taking a deep breath. "We should have discussed things beforehand. I didn't mean to lead you…" Lead him where? "Anywhere. I didn't think at all." Not of him. She'd thought of *her* desires, *her* apprehension, only her. "I behaved selfishly."

"My body would beg to differ," he said wryly.

While she appreciated his sense of humor, she wasn't sure it was appropriate here. Not when she was trying to apologize for what had amounted to an unforgettable night. "Yes, it was pleasant. However, you must see the truth—you need an heir. I can't give you one."

"My cousin, though now gone, had a son. He's still very young, but he will inherit if I don't have chil-dren. I don't know him—or his mother—at all. How-ever, regardless of whether I have an heir, it seems you would prefer a husband who already has children."

Her chest pinched. "I don't even know if I want to wed."

"It's a conundrum." His tone was quiet and perhaps sad. "I do understand. Nothing, however, changes how much I enjoyed last night. Or how much I'd like to do it again."

Her gaze shot to his. "Please don't say that." Because she wanted it too. Yet, there was no point to it, except to cause heartache.

"Why? Is it wrong to seek pleasure? To want to enjoy ourselves together?"

Before she could answer, they were joined by Lord Rotherham. Tall, with blond hair and brilliant green eyes, the earl asked which biscuit he should choose.

Edmund pointed to their shared favorite. "This one. Unless you'd rather try something less delicious in case you end up liking it too much." He shot her a testy stare before taking himself away from the table and leaving her alone with Rotherham.

Realizing she was frowning after him, she blinked and smoothed her expression before turning her attention to the attractive earl. He flashed her his almost ever-present wicked smile before he nibbled at the biscuit.

"Oh, that is good," he said around the bite in his mouth. He swallowed. "I adore lemon. So tart and sweet at once. I believe Howell says that's what he looks for in a lady."

"And what do you look for?" Genie asked, purposely flirting. Her reasons were twofold. First, to distract anyone from thinking she and Edmund were a pair. There had been a few mumblings, and she wanted to quash them. She didn't want to be linked to anyone. Second, to dissuade Edmund from pursuing anything between them. Last night had been wonderful, but it was a single occurrence and wouldn't be repeated.

"I suppose there's nothing wrong with sweet and tart, though I might choose spice as a better description." He narrowed his eyes slightly at her. "How would you describe your taste in gentlemen?"

Genie's gaze involuntarily flicked toward Edmund. She didn't particularly want to answer that question. Thankfully, they were joined by Mr. Sterling.

"We're discussing the biscuits," Genie said. "I like the lavender lemon variety. Do you have a favorite?"

"Almond. Lavender is awful." Sterling made a face as he reached for an almond one. "My eldest daughter would agree with you. We often debate the true purpose of lavender. I insist it's for fragrance only. As a flavor, it's an abomination. She argues with me incessantly."

Rotherham laughed as he took one of the lavender lemon biscuits. "That sounds like my daughters. Sometimes I think they like to argue with me just to be contrary."

"Yes!" Sterling agreed, his dark blue eyes sparking with mirth.

Genie didn't laugh along with them. How could she when she would give anything for a contrary daughter? "They all sound charming."

"Your son is grown now, but surely he was difficult at some point?" Sterling asked before taking a bite of his almond biscuit.

"My stepson, yes." Titus had been a horrible rake for a few years before his father died. That was rather different from arguing over herbs. "I think there is always difficulty in being a parent." A particular difficulty that was at once rife with joy and pain. She would never trade her three years with Eliza even if she'd known the heartbreak she would endure.

"That is true," Rotherham said. "Why do you think there are so many people looking to remarry at this party?" He laughed. "Doing this alone is too hard."

Genie didn't know from experience, but Jerome

had said the same thing before they'd wed. He'd wanted to remarry as soon as possible—for Titus. Still, he'd been adamant about finding love the second time and had been overjoyed to find Genie, who'd met both his needs and his desires.

She looked between the two men. "What is more important to you—finding a mother for your children or finding a wife for yourself?"

Sterling, who was clearly interested in her but who had also made self-deprecating remarks about being a mere mister while she was a dowager duchess and daughter of a viscount, gestured with the biscuit between his fingers. "Ideally, I'd find both." He popped the rest of the biscuit into his mouth.

Rotherham seemed to think for a moment. "Honestly? I adore my daughters. Losing their mother was hard. Finding someone with whom they can hopefully form a close relationship is what will make me happy. So that is my answer." He finished his biscuit.

Genie couldn't help but melt a bit at his words. "That's lovely," she said softly. Perhaps he wasn't *too* young for her?

Wait, was she suddenly on the hunt for a husband? Or was she looking to be a mother? It would be best if she wanted both—as Sterling had said. She looked to him. "I think you have the right of it. Kendal and I were fortunate to have both."

"You liked being a stepmother?" Sterling asked.

"I do. Kendal—my stepson—is everything to me."

Both men looked at her as if they were envisioning her in that role. She suddenly felt uncomfortable.

"The sun has come out!" Cecilia said loudly. Everyone turned toward the windows. "Let us prepare for the ride. We'll congregate at the stables in one hour."

People began leaving the drawing room, eager to

change into their riding clothes and get outside. Genie had to admit she was looking forward to some fresh air on her face. Perhaps she could forget about the complexities of this party for a while.

Before departing, both men said they looked forward to seeing her on the ride. As Genie made her way to the door, Cecilia approached her.

"I thought you and Satterfield were perhaps forming an attachment, but then I've seen you with Sterling several times. And I just saw you flirting with Rotherham." Cecilia grinned. "This is precisely what I was hoping for when I invited you. I do hope one of them will suit you."

One had, at least in a particular area. Genie pushed thoughts of Edmund and his…skills from her mind. "I still haven't quite forgiven you for not telling me the purpose of this party in advance. But I am having a good time." She smiled to take the sting from the first part.

Cecilia gave her a sheepish look. "I should have told you, but was I wrong in thinking you would not have come?"

Genie sighed. "Probably not. However, I would ask that you not be too eager about pairing me off. Just because I'm enjoying myself doesn't mean I'm ready to marry again."

"All right, but there are plenty of gentlemen to choose from. Sterling would be a good match. You don't care that he doesn't have a title, do you?"

"Of course not."

Waving her hand, Cecilia said, "I didn't think so."

"It seems as though your matchmaking efforts will bear fruit. There are at least a pair or two, from what I'm hearing." Genie didn't like gossip, but in a party of this size, it was impossible to ignore comments that were made.

Cecilia clasped her hands together. "I do hope so!

I'm wondering if I should make this an annual event. Why not?"

"Indeed, why not." Genie arched a brow at her cousin. "Provided you make it clear to every guest what to expect."

Laughing, Cecilia put her arm through Genie's. "Yes, yes. Now, let us don our riding costumes and show everyone how well our grandfather insisted we learn to ride."

Genie laughed with her, remembering their summers together at their grandfather's estate. "Thank you for inviting me. I don't regret coming."

Nor did she regret visiting Edmund last night. It might have been better if she hadn't, but Genie would forever be grateful that she did.

CHAPTER 8

*N*ot even a brisk ride across Blickton's extensive parkland had eased the frustration roiling inside Edmund. That Genie had apologized to him for what had happened last night rankled him horribly. He regretted nothing—there was nothing to apologize for.

Then he'd had to watch her laugh and smile with bloody Rotherham, who was far too good-looking than any man had a right to be, *and* with Sterling, who'd been trailing after her all week. It was enough to drive a man to drink. Or to surrender to his inner beast and snatch the fair damsel from her horse, then ride off with her into the wilds. The latter plan, despite its barbarity, held a tantalizing appeal.

Nevertheless, Edmund returned to the stable yard with the rest of the guests and then lingered with the gentlemen as the ladies made their way inside. He watched Genie go, her backside swaying, tempting him to reveal his inner savagery. He recalled sliding his hand beneath her as he'd feasted between her thighs, his fingers closing around her soft flesh, and began to grow hard.

Dammit.

He turned away, burying a scowl.

The men were discussing which women were the best riders. Mrs. Sheldon was far and away superior, but Genie and her cousin, their hostess, were both excellent. Poor Mrs. Wynne-Hargest had struggled, but Sir Nathaniel had been kind enough to lend her assistance. So much so that they were now rumored to be a pair. He demurred, refusing to confirm nor deny any attachment.

Cosford sent a sly look toward Rotherham. "I'd thought you might be fixated on Mrs. Dunthorpe, but after today, I think it might be the dowager duchess."

Rotherham rolled his eyes. "Give it up, Cosford. No one is going to come out and say whom they're sleeping with or courting or anything else." There was a rousing chorus of agreement.

"Besides, it's obvious Her Grace is interested in Sterling," Howell said, elbowing Sterling, who stood beside him.

Edmund's irritation reached a boiling point, and he strode from the group. Not toward the house, but back to the stable, where he intended to help put away the tack. When he was unsettled, he always turned to manual labor to relax and reset his equilibrium. Or sex.

Since he had no hope for the latter, he would take the labor.

At first, the grooms attempted to decline his offer of assistance, but he ultimately convinced them to let him stay. He removed his coat and threw himself into the work, enjoying every moment, including the camaraderie of the grooms and stable lads. It wasn't terribly seemly for an earl to behave in this manner, but he didn't care. His own stable men knew to expect him and indeed welcomed him.

After some time, he felt refreshed. He bid goodbye to the grooms, picked up his coat, and went back into the yard, which was now thankfully empty. Intending to don his coat before returning to the house, he caught sight of something in the grass glinting in the sun.

He bent to pick the object up—an earring. Which he recognized. The gold-and-carnelian piece belonged to Genie.

His pulse quickened at the prospect of returning it to her. If only she hadn't asked him not to say he'd enjoyed last night. He'd been certain she'd enjoyed it too. But it seemed she regretted it.

He closed his fist around the earring and straightened. Looking toward the house, he was surprised to see the object of his thoughts coming directly toward him.

Genie slowed as she neared him. She looked about on the ground. "I lost an earring."

He held out his hand, opening his fist. "This one?"

She sucked in a breath. "Yes. Thank you."

He closed his hand around it once more. "I could hold it hostage."

Her gaze snapped to his, her eyes widening. "For what?"

"Do you regret what happened last night?" He had to know, and yet he didn't think he could bear it if she said yes.

It took her a moment to respond, but it was worth the wait. "No." She cautiously stepped toward him. "Still, I don't wish to repeat it."

"Why not?"

"Edmund, please don't do this. It's best if we move on."

He took her hand and pivoted, pulling her with him behind the stable. Not pulling, exactly, because she wasn't resisting.

When they were out of sight of the house, he let go of her and turned to face her. "Why? Tell me why you want to pretend there isn't something between us."

"I did!" Her eyes blistered with fire. "We don't want the same things. We can't make each other happy, not past this party."

They *didn't* want the same things. She wanted children, and he didn't have any. He needed an heir, and she couldn't give him one. That was the difference—she wanted and he needed. But did he want a child? He'd thought he might, but at the moment, he couldn't see past the strong feelings he had for her.

He *wanted* every moment with her he could get. Even if this was to be the last one. "Then why not make the most of this party while we're here? Come to me tonight."

"No."

He swore. Reaching for her hand, he put the earring in her palm. "Take this and go, then."

She stared at the jewel. Shaking, she brought it up to her ear and slid it through the tiny hole, fastening it in place. But she didn't go. She stood there, her chest heaving as she stared at him.

He saw the conflict in her eyes—the desire, the pain. "Genie, my darling, why do you fight this?" He gently stroked her jaw, then cupped her cheek.

"I can't be the woman you need."

His heart ached at the anguish in her voice. "You are the woman I *want*." And he knew in that moment, despite the brevity of their acquaintance and the stark conflict that would seem to prevent their future, she was.

She put her hands on his shoulders and kissed him. Edmund snaked his arm around her waist, pulling her chest against his. He slanted his mouth over hers and made certain she knew how badly he wanted her. Needed her. Desired her above all others.

He tossed his coat and hat away, then nipped her lower lip and kissed along her jawline, licking her flesh toward her ear. Dragging his mouth along her neck, he savored her taste and scent.

"Edmund, I—"

He pulled his head up and looked into her hazy eyes. "What? Tell me what you want. If you want me to go, I will. If you want me to toss up your skirts and shag you senseless, I will. *Tell me*, Genie."

"Take me. Now. *Please*." She dug her fingers into his neck and shoulders.

He steered her backward until she met the exterior of the stable. They were somewhat obscured by a shrub on one side, but if someone happened by on the other, they would be seen. "Be sure you want this —here. Now." He clasped her hip and ground against her.

She whimpered. "Yes." She tugged at her skirts, raising them.

There was nothing to aid them. He would have to lift her, but knew he could. Hell, he could have carried the damn world if it meant he could share ecstasy with her one more time.

He put his hand on hers and brought her skirts to her waist. "Hold them," he instructed before he kissed her again. She clutched at his head, her tongue dancing wildly with his.

Edmund slipped his hand between her legs and stroked her satiny flesh. She was soft and wet. Ready. And he was unbearably hard for her. He played with her, pressing her clitoris and sliding his finger into her sheath. She clenched around him, gasping into his mouth.

Then her hands were on his fall, unbuttoning him and pulling his cock free. She encircled him with her hand, stroking him from base to tip over and over until he feared he would spill himself in her hand.

"Enough," he rasped. "Hold on to me."

She curled her hands around his neck, and he lifted her against the stable. "Wrap your legs around me." She did as he instructed. "Good girl."

Laughing softly, she said, "I am not a girl."

"No, you are not. You're the most desirable woman I've ever known." He clasped his cock and guided himself to her pussy. He held her backside as he moved into her, sheathing himself entirely.

Resting against her, he exhaled and closed his eyes. She felt so damn good around him, so right. He didn't think anything in his life had been this perfect, and he somehow knew nothing ever would be.

"Genie," he whispered, kissing her temple, her cheek, her lips.

She dug her heels into his backside. "Edmund, please. *Move.*"

"Tell me what you want, Genie." He kissed her hard and fast. "Should I go slow?" He rotated his hips against hers in a dizzyingly sedate fashion. His blood rushed through his ears, urging him to go faster. "Or should I shag you senseless, as I said?"

She tipped her head back and moaned softly, then leaned forward and snagged his earlobe with her teeth. "Hard. Fast. Make me come, Edmund."

Edmund nearly spilled himself. Where was the hesitant, almost shy, dowager? He didn't care. He was desperate for this Genie—no, he wanted every aspect of her. He clutched her backside and put his other hand on the side of her head, his fingers digging into her hair beneath her hat. "Look at me, Genie."

She focused her eyes on his, and he was lost in the desire blazing in their depths. He thrust into her again and again, increasing his pace until he thundered into her.

Her eyes slitted, and she cried out.

"Shh." He kissed her, taking her moans and whimpers into himself. Each sound increased his drive, pushing him to the precipice. His orgasm gathered. He was so close. He tore his mouth from hers and dragged it to her ear. "Come with me, Genie. *Now.*"

Her muscles tightened around him, and he felt her shudder. It was all he needed to let go. In a torrent of need and passion, he drove deep into her and came, somehow managing not to shout his divine satisfaction.

He held her tightly as their bodies moved together in bliss and desperation. And finally, their tension eased as release washed over them. He held her still, his cheek pressed to hers as he gulped in breath after breath to calm his racing heart.

Kissing her jaw, he lowered her gently to the ground. She unwrapped her legs from his waist and stood against the stable. Her skirts dropped, covering her once more. Edmund put himself back together, tucking his cock into his smallclothes and buttoning his fall.

Genie looked toward the house. "That was dangerous."

"Perhaps that's what made it so delightful." Edmund couldn't help but smile. "That, and you."

She turned her head to look at him, her eyes wide and her cheeks gorgeously flushed. He wanted to look at her like that for the rest of his days.

"This changes nothing." She smoothed her hands over her skirts as she took a deep breath.

The frustration he'd banished working in the stable—and from shagging her—rose in him again. "You can't deny there is something between us. Do you really want to ignore it?"

"We must." She looked at him imploringly. "Edmund, this is not enough."

"If you mean sex, there is more than that between us, and you know it. I feel as though I'm holding my breath every moment you aren't in my sight. Anticipation ravages me until you walk into the room and brighten the world."

Her gaze softened as her lips parted. "Edmund. But knowing what we do, this is folly."

He felt as though he'd been punched in the gut. "It isn't to me."

Her forehead gathered into worried little pleats. "I'm sorry." Then she turned and hurried back toward the house.

He considered following her but didn't. This wasn't something he could force. Perhaps she didn't reciprocate his feelings. He'd wanted her for twenty years. In truth, he'd moved on from her long ago, after she'd wed Kendal. He'd never imagined having a chance, and he certainly hadn't come to this party with the intention of seeing her, let alone pursuing her.

This was the realization of a dream from his youth and nothing more. He'd taken a different path and should stay on it—find a wife now who would suit his needs. That meant an heir.

There were several viable women here. Women without children who might yet bear fruit, and women with children who had proven their ability to give him what he needed.

That sounded so cold and callous, but it was the way of things, particularly for a man of his station. Marrying for love was a luxury most didn't achieve. Why should he think he was special?

Edmund went to pick up his coat and pulled it on. Then he slammed his hat on his head. Ignoring the hollow ache spreading inside him, he stalked toward the house, intent on downing an entire bottle of brandy if he must. Whatever it took to forget about Genie.

~

*N*ursing a slight headache the following morning, Edmund was late to breakfast. When he arrived, the only seat available was between Lady Bradford and Mrs. Grey. He immediately regretted his decision to come downstairs.

Lady Bradford slid him a curious look and whispered, "Are you still drunk?"

"No." He'd been rather intoxicated when she'd come to his room last night looking for an assignation.

"Well, you look terrible."

"Thank you." He nudged the food he'd obtained from the sideboard around his plate with his fork.

Cosford stood at the head of the table. "It's my pleasure to make an announcement this morning." He looked to his left at the couple seated there. "It is my distinct honor to share the engagement of Lord Audlington and Mrs. Sheldon!"

Applause and cheers sounded from around the table. Rotherham lifted his glass of ale. "A toast to the betrothed couple!"

Everyone raised their glasses and called, "Huzzah!"

Edmund sipped his ale as the noise of everyone's reactions caused his head to throb.

"I wonder who will be next?" Lady Cosford said from the other end of the table near Edmund.

He glanced toward Genie across the table next to Lord Audlington, who was gazing besottedly at his betrothed. Genie was staring at her plate.

"My money is on Mrs. Fitzwarren and Sir Godwin," Lord Pritchard said with a grin.

"Now, now," Lady Cosford said, pursing her lips. "Let us not speculate. It's incredibly…awkward."

"I'll take that bet," Mrs. Hatcliff-Lind said, with a

ruthless glint in her eye and a smile pulling at her lips.

"Excellent!" Pritchard turned to their host. "Cosford, will you take down bets?"

Lady Cosford waved her hand. "No, no, we can't do that!"

Cosford coughed. "You heard our intrepid hostess." He glanced toward Pritchard, and the look they exchanged said the wagers would absolutely happen, just in secret.

"Well, if they are going to take wagers, I will bet on you and Lady Bradford," Mrs. Grey whispered from his right.

Edmund swung his head around to look at her. "What?"

"I won't be the only one," she said, her blue eyes probing his. "Someone saw Lady Bradford outside your chamber last night."

Hell and the devil. She *had* come to his chamber, but he'd turned her away. He'd been far too soused to invite a lady to his bed. More importantly, he didn't want anyone but Genie.

His gaze strayed toward her. She was watching him intently, her mouth drawn into a judgmental frown. Damn. Had she heard the rumor about Lady Bradford?

Swearing silently, Edmund picked up his ale and took a long drink. It didn't matter what she'd heard or what she thought. She'd been very clear—even after they'd shared that amazing shag behind the stable yesterday.

He stood abruptly from the table and quit the dining room. He had one more day to suffer this infernal party, and then he could get back to his life. The one that hadn't included Genie and never would.

CHAPTER 9

One month later, Lakemoor Dower House

enie set the letter aside and looked out at the gray afternoon. The dismal sky matched her mood. Another batch of letters from friends —and a potential suitor. Not one of them was from Edmund, nor had there been one from him since the house party.

Did she really expect him to write? Despite the intimacy they'd shared, they'd left things with an air of finality. Furthermore, she'd departed early.

After their tryst behind the stable, she'd somehow made it through dinner that night, even though she couldn't stop thinking of Edmund—his smile, his easygoing nature, the way he made her feel. After dinner, there had been dancing, which had led to a mishap in which Lettie had fallen into Edmund's arms. They'd laughed and seemed to hold on to one another for a bit longer than necessary. Coupling that with the rumor that Lettie had visited his room the night before, Genie had convinced herself that it was for the best if he pursued Lettie. Or someone else.

Anyone but her.

She glanced at the last letter she'd read. It was from Mr. Sterling. He'd written to her three times since the party, and in this letter, he'd asked if he could visit. He was kind, warm, and effusive in his flattery—maybe even a little too much—and clearly in want of a wife. Or, more importantly, a mother for his children.

She'd half expected to hear from Lord Rotherham too, but had not. Perhaps he'd deemed her too old after all. Especially since, with two daughters, he was still in need of an heir. Like Edmund.

A movement outside caught Genie's attention. Her stepson, Titus, strode up the walkway to the front door of the dower house. She stood and heard her butler greet him a moment later.

Summoning a smile as Titus walked into the sitting room, she bade him enter. "Do you want tea?"

He shook his head. "No, thank you. I just got back from a ride and thought I'd stop in. Reading correspondence?" He looked toward the desk behind her in front of the window.

She glanced over her shoulder. "Yes."

Titus's brow puckered. It was an expression that made him look so much like his father that Genie never failed to feel a tick in her chest. With black hair, sharp green eyes, and a tall, fit form, he was an exceptionally handsome man. And at twenty-four, with a ducal title and multiple estates, he was a sought-after match on the Marriage Mart. Or he would be if he put himself in any situations that would give a young lady the impression he was interested in taking a wife.

He was not.

"I hope you'll forgive my impertinence," he said.

"You've been...different since you returned from the house party. I assumed it was due to missing Father. I can't imagine it was easy to be at a social event with other married couples."

Genie hadn't told him about the party at all. He'd taken a trip to one of his other estates a few days after she'd returned and had been gone a fortnight. "Actually, the only married couple in attendance were our hosts."

His brows shot up. "Indeed?"

Genie sat in her favorite chair and gestured for him to take a seat. He dropped onto the settee and stretched his long legs out in front of him.

"My cousin conceived of the party as a way for widows and widowers as well as unmarried gentleman to...socialize."

He looked confused. "Was it a matchmaking enterprise?"

"Somewhat—but not all the matches were necessarily meant to be permanent. If you catch my meaning."

Titus's lips stretched into a smile. "I do. Diabolically brilliant." He sobered and pulled his legs up. "You didn't care for it?"

"She didn't tell me the purpose in advance, which I found disappointing. I did not appreciate being surprised. In fact, I wanted to leave immediately, but the rain washed out the road."

"I can't believe you didn't tell me this before."

She hadn't meant to keep it from him. Generally, they were quite open with each other. But the party had surprised her in many ways, and she was still trying to determine how to proceed.

"I am not sure what to say." She folded her hands in her lap. "I suppose I didn't want you to think I'd moved on from your father."

"Have you?" He exhaled. "Never mind—that's

none of my business. I *hope* you have, actually. He wanted that."

She'd never discussed this with him. "How do you know?"

He gave her a sheepish look. "You know he left me letters. One of them was about you. He urged me to encourage you to marry again. He argued you are much too young to remain alone." He paused for a moment, resting his elbow on the arm of the settee. "I tend to agree with him, but it's entirely up to you. I will support whatever you wish—always."

Genie felt such love for this boy—no, man. She supposed he would always be the sweet five-year-old she'd promised to raise as her son when she'd wed his father.

"Did you...meet someone?" Titus asked, pulling Genie back to the present.

There was no reason not to tell him the truth. "I did. However, we didn't suit." She glanced toward the desk again. "Another gentleman from the party has been writing to me. There's a chance *we* may suit, however." Saying the words out loud made her doubt the possibility. Thinking of Peter Sterling didn't give her the same rush of anticipation that thinking of Edmund did. She realized she missed him dreadfully—his surreptitious heated looks in her direction, his deep laugh, his care and concern for her well-being.

He cocked his head. "Forgive me again, but you don't sound very enthusiastic."

"I'm not entirely certain I'm ready to wed again. Now or perhaps ever. I'm not sure I can bring myself to leave Lakemoor. Or you." She gave him a tremulous smile.

He leaned forward. "You must make decisions that are best for you. I will be fine." He glanced away, then met her gaze once more. "You haven't asked for my advice, but I hope you will pursue what makes you happy. If anyone deserves joy, it's you."

"Thank you." She instantly thought of Edmund. The time they'd spent together had been her happiest moments since Jerome had died.

Her butler appeared in the doorway. He looked to Genie. "Your Grace, a gentleman has arrived to see you."

Her breath snagged and her heart sped. No, it wouldn't be Edmund. But how she wished it was. She realized in that moment that she'd fallen quite desperately in love with him. Probably. How could she be sure when she'd only ever loved one other person?

Because the sensation was similar. She missed Edmund. She thought of him all the time. She yearned to see him again. And now that a gentleman had arrived, she fervently hoped it was him even as she knew it wouldn't be.

The butler added, "Mr. Peter Sterling."

Genie's belly sank. "Show him in."

Titus started to rise. "Shall I go?"

"No, stay, if you don't mind. He will have come a long way. Can he stay at the house tonight?"

"Of course." He settled back onto the settee.

Mr. Sterling came into the sitting room. His dark blue eyes settled on her, and he smiled warmly. Then his gaze landed on Titus, and he seemed to freeze for a moment.

"Welcome, Mr. Sterling," Genie said. "Come in and join us. Allow me to present my stepson, the Duke of Kendal."

Mr. Sterling bowed. "Your Grace, I am pleased to make your acquaintance."

"As am I yours," Titus said. "Please, sit." He gestured to a vacant chair near Genie.

Mr. Sterling walked to the chair and slowly lowered himself. "I beg your pardon for arriving unannounced." He looked to Genie. "Perhaps you received my letter?"

"Just today, in fact. I was going to respond that I would be delighted to have you visit." What could she say now that he was here? She flicked a glance at Titus and saw a slight scowl marring his forehead, reminding her again of Jerome.

Mr. Sterling's features creased in a brief grimace. "I took that chance. I'm so glad it was the right one."

"You've come an awfully long way. Kendal will arrange for your room at the manor house."

"That would be most welcome, thank you." Mr. Sterling inclined his head toward Titus.

"I'll go and see to that." Titus stood. "Dinner will be at six." He sent Genie a questioning look, and she responded with the barest shake of her head. This wasn't the man she wanted.

And she *did* want a man.

"See you later," Titus said before departing.

Genie drew a deep breath. She needed to tell Mr. Sterling that she was not interested in a courtship or marriage.

"Are you certain it's all right that I've come?" Mr. Sterling asked.

"Yes. As you can imagine, I haven't had many visitors here." That was certainly true, and while she didn't want to marry Mr. Sterling, she'd enjoyed his company and conversation at Blickton.

"You can probably guess why I've come. It's an awfully long journey just to pay a visit."

It was indeed, since he lived a few days' ride from the Lake District. As to why he'd come…yes, she could guess. But she didn't want to. "Why *have* you come?"

He frowned slightly. "I found we suited well at Blickton. I enjoyed our time together very much. I thought you felt the same."

The fact that he kept talking about what he felt and thought without *asking*—and instead assuming—how she felt and thought grated on her nerves, but she pushed that away. She already knew he wasn't right for her.

"The house party was most pleasant. Since you have come this far, I am led to believe you wish to continue our relationship."

He brightened. "I do indeed. I—my goodness, this is more difficult than I anticipated. I've only done this once before, and I was quite young and silly. I must admit, I feel rather silly in this moment." He laughed nervously. "Or apprehensive." He slid from the chair and got onto one knee before her. "Your Grace, I would be honored if you would be my wife. I promise to care for you the rest of my days, and I know my children will admire and care for you as much as I do."

His children. Genie couldn't ignore the pang of longing that came with the thought of mothering more children. She couldn't do that with Edmund. And he needed children. Or at least one child—an heir.

She couldn't contemplate a future with Edmund. It didn't matter that she loved him. He needed an heir, and she couldn't give him one. That was the beginning and the end of it.

But here was a man who cared for her, with four children in need of a mother. It would be a nice life. She'd married for love once, and that was more than many people experienced.

She smiled at him. "I am so humbled by your proposal, Mr. Sterling. Would it be all right if I thought about it tonight and gave you an answer on the morrow? In the meantime, we will dine with my stepson and spend the evening together. If that's acceptable to you."

His shoulders dipped as he relaxed, a smile of relief breaking over his features. "More than acceptable. You are a woman of exceeding good humor and charm."

How could she find fault with that?

CHAPTER 10

"*Y*ou're up early," Cosford said as Edmund entered the dining room at Rotherham's hunting lodge near Lancaster. "Especially given last night's activities." He chuckled before sipping his coffee.

Edmund filled his plate from the sideboard and joined Cosford at the table. "I didn't imbibe as much as you—or Rotherham."

A footman came forward and offered coffee or ale. Edmund took both.

"I don't think anyone imbibed as much as Rotherham," Cosford said, wincing. "He's been in a bit of a state, hasn't he?"

"Has he?" Edmund hadn't noticed. Probably because he'd been in his own "state." A state of pining for a woman he couldn't have. And when he wasn't pining, he vacillated between anger at the way Genie had left Blickton without saying goodbye and mourning for what he'd had—briefly—and lost.

"I suppose you haven't been paying attention." Cosford cut a piece of ham. "Too wrapped up in your own melancholy."

"I am not melancholy." Edmund thought he'd done a fair job of hiding his distraction.

Cosford swallowed his bite of ham. "You forget that the party was at *my* house. And that my wife misses nothing. Well, almost nothing. Also that she is Genie's—sorry, the dowager duchess's—cousin."

Hell. Had Genie told Lady Cosford something? "What are you getting at, Cosford?"

Lifting a shoulder, Cosford picked up his coffee. "I know you were visited by another woman besides Lady Bradford. I wasn't entirely sure who it was, but then one of the stableboys saw you and Genie after our ride." He didn't need to say what the boy had seen, and they both knew it.

Edmund scooped some eggs from his plate into his mouth and avoided looking at Cosford.

"When Genie left early," Cosford continued, "we assumed something had broken down between you. Cecilia was quite upset."

What had Genie told them? "I didn't know she was leaving," Edmund said, reaching for the ale and taking a long pull.

Cosford's brows climbed his forehead. "You didn't?" He angled his head. "She surprised us after breakfast that morning when she said she was going to depart. Cecilia had hoped her cousin would find a match. My wife believes her cousin isn't happy unless she has someone to care for, and her stepson is old enough to manage without her, of course."

Edmund didn't know what he could say to that. He'd love for Genie to care for him—and he for her.

"She's had too much sadness," Cosford said, shaking his head. "But I suspect you know that."

He did. She'd lost her daughter, her husband, and the hope for more children of her own. Edmund had heard the anguish in her voice when she'd told him of Eliza.

Edmund tried to eat, but his appetite was waning. He drank coffee instead.

"Anyway, it seems you and she did not match. But seeing you here, I wonder if you hoped you might."

"I thought it was a possibility, but it is not."

Cosford exhaled as he reached for a slice of toast. "It's just as well. Sterling confided to Cecilia that he planned to propose to Genie. He was effusive in his appreciation for Cecilia bringing them together at the party.

Jealousy seared through Edmund, blistering him with a regret he'd never known. Twenty years ago, he'd seen Genie and accepted that they were not to be. She'd been the diamond of the Season, poised to marry well, and he'd been on the verge of his Grand Tour. When he'd encountered her at the house party, it seemed Fate had given him a second chance.

Until it became frankly apparent that they were at cross purposes. It was grossly unfair. The infatuation he'd felt for her twenty years ago had bloomed into full-blown love, and he was almost certain she'd at least begun to feel the same. Or maybe it had just been a stunning mutual attraction—quick to burn and just as fast to turn to ash.

There was only one way for him to know. He had to tell her exactly how he felt and what he wanted. If she didn't feel the same, then he would at least know for certain.

And what if she loved him, but not enough to forgo children? What about his earldom?

"I have an heir."

"What's that?" Cosford asked, blinking.

Edmund realized he'd spoken his thoughts aloud. "The dowager duchess and I decided we didn't suit because I need an heir." She also wanted to be a mother again, and a widower with children could make that happen. Edmund wouldn't share that with Cosford, however.

"You just said you have one."

"I do indeed." No, the boy wasn't his offspring, and he'd have to plan for the child to be the presumptive heir. Could he accept never having a child of his own? If it meant a life with Genie, yes.

None of that, however, solved the problem of Genie's desire for more children.

Cosford gave him a pointed look. "Sterling plans to propose soon."

Edmund pushed back his chair and stood. Whether she would accept him or not, he had to tell Genie the truth of his feelings for her. "Then I'd best be on my way. I'm going to leave immediately and have my coach follow." He'd brought his own horse and would use him to get to Lakemoor as quickly as possible.

Cosford leaned back in his chair and smiled. "Cecilia will be pleased. She was hoping for you over Sterling."

"We'll see what Genie is hoping for." Edmund couldn't believe what a fool he'd been. He wouldn't lose her this time.

He prayed he wasn't too late.

❧

*A*fter spending a lovely evening with Peter—Mr. Sterling had insisted she call him by his first name—Genie was more torn than ever. She'd been unable to sleep until late into the night.

But then she'd awakened with a remarkable clarity: if she loved Edmund, why would she consider marrying another? Because Peter had children? Genie did too. She had a stepson—a son—she loved more than anything.

Edmund, however, did not. Would he consider a future with her knowing she couldn't give him a child? She wouldn't blame him if he couldn't. Even so, she didn't think she could live with herself if she didn't tell him how she felt.

Which meant she had to see him. Right away. Now that she knew what she wanted, what she *must* do, she couldn't wait. Unfortunately, his estate was two days away at least, if the weather cooperated.

First, however, she had to give Peter her answer to his proposal. He would be here shortly. In the meantime, she instructed her maid to pack for a trip and asked her butler to inform the stable to prepare her coach.

When Peter arrived, she greeted him in the sitting room as she'd done the day before. He kissed her hand and looked at her expectantly. "I don't wish to press you for a decision, but I am ever hopeful."

"I told you I would have an answer today, and I do." She turned toward the seating area and gestured to the settee. "Shall we sit?"

She went to stand in front of her chair, and he moved to the settee. He seemed to realize she wasn't going to sit beside him, because he glanced at the settee and then her chair and frowned.

Genie sat down, and he followed, slowly sinking to the settee. She'd rehearsed what to say, but the words flew from her mind. "Mr. Sterling—Peter. I'm afraid I must refuse your wonderful proposal."

His frown returned and deepened. "If it's wonderful, why would you refuse it?"

Oh dear, was he going to be difficult? No, she would give him the benefit of the doubt. He would be disappointed, of course. "Because I love another." It was the truth, and she saw no reason to lie. "It is no fault of yours, I assure you. If not for…this other person, I believe I would have accepted your proposal."

Yes, she would have. Cecilia was right—she didn't like being alone.

He pressed his lips together, his eyes darkening as

he averted his gaze toward the window. At length, he said, "I see. I am disappointed."

"For that, I am sorry."

"Your letters were rather encouraging," he said with a hint of accusation.

Damn, apparently he *was* going to be difficult. She wanted to be on her way!

"I thought we might suit, but I realized yesterday that I have deep feelings for someone else. I would have communicated that to you in my next letter—instead of inviting you to visit, which you did anyway." She let her own accusation float in the air between them.

"Yes, and it was quite a journey."

"I'm sorry you regret coming."

"It isn't that." He took a breath and exhaled. Then he seemed to...pout. "I regret that you do not return my affection."

Affection? Still no mention of love. Genie was incredibly relieved she hadn't accepted his proposal. She acknowledged it was foolish to think she could marry twice for love, but she didn't think she could wed for any other reason. She thought of what Lady Clinton had said about her two different marriages—one for love and one for convenience—and knew she couldn't do that.

"You deserve someone who does." Genie rose, eager to end the visit. She didn't see any reason to prolong things.

He slowly got to his feet. "Well, I am shocked by your answer." He narrowed one eye at her. "Are you certain?"

"I am."

"What if this fellow doesn't love you in return? My offer would still remain."

Oh, he was *really* being difficult! "That is most kind of you, but I won't change my mind," she said firmly. "I do appreciate you coming all this way, and I'm sorry things aren't different." She cringed inwardly because she wasn't. She had been earlier, but now, she was quite ready to see Mr. Sterling's back as he left.

He hesitated a moment, then finally said, "Good day, Your Grace."

"Have a safe journey, Mr. Sterling." Genie watched as he turned and departed the sitting room.

Not wanting to waste a moment, Genie dashed from the room. She would leave as soon as possible. Now that she knew what she wanted, she was anxious to pursue her heart's desire.

Hopefully, Edmund felt the same, but she resolved to understand if the obstacles between them were too great. She prayed they were not—and that she hadn't completely botched things at Blickton. It was entirely possible she had. For that, she had no one to blame but herself.

~

A groom ran to meet Edmund as he rode to the front of the Duke of Kendal's magnificent manor house on his estate, Lakemoor. The afternoon sun streaming through the clouds bathed the brown stone in mottled but warm light. He'd been grateful for the fair weather, which had made for a speedy trip, particularly since he'd cut across fields the last several miles.

"Please take good care of him," Edmund said to the groom. "We've ridden hard." He stroked his horse's nose and murmured words of appreciation and affection.

The lad nodded. "I will, sir."

Edmund turned and strode to the door, which the butler held open. "The Earl of Satterfield to see the

Duke," Edmund said as he removed his hat and gloves.

The butler took his accessories. "I don't believe he is expecting you, my lord."

"He was not. Nevertheless, I am here."

"Of course. Come with me." The butler led Edmund to a large, well-appointed room. "If you'll just wait here, I'll inform His Grace you have arrived."

Anticipation curled through Edmund. Anxiety had driven him to ride hard and fast, and now that he was here, he was keen to see Genie, but also apprehensive. She might still refuse him.

He prowled the room, and his gaze fell on the painting above the mantel. His breath halted, as did his feet. Captured in her youth, Genie stared back at him, a warm smile curving her lush mouth. But she wasn't alone. Beside her, and just a bit behind, stood her husband. His gaze was on her—as it should be. The artist had perfectly captured the love in his eyes.

How could Edmund compete with that?

"Welcome, Lord Satterfield."

Edmund turned from the beautiful portrait and saw the young duke striding into the room. "Thank you for seeing me." They'd met before, of course. Edmund had specifically introduced himself when Kendal had taken his father's seat in the Lords. He'd offered his assistance and guidance if Kendal ever needed it. Edmund had wanted to provide support in the way Kendal's father had done for him.

And now Edmund was stealing his former mentor's wife. That was absurd. He couldn't steal her, not from a dead man. He glanced back at the painting and silently said, *I love her. I will take care of her. If she'll have me.*

There was, of course, no response, just a man staring at his beloved for all time.

"How can I be of service?" Kendal asked. "Shall we

sit? Would you care for refreshment? I don't know how far you've come, but my butler said you rode up on a horse that looked as if it had seen some miles."

"Indeed. I came from near Lancaster. I wanted to arrive before dark."

Kendal smiled. "You've done that with time to spare." He took one of the chairs and gestured for Edmund to sit.

But Edmund didn't want to. He wanted to see Genie. The only reason he hadn't gone straight to the dower house was because he didn't know precisely where it was. Also, and mostly, so he could speak with Kendal before he saw her.

"Forgive me if I don't sit. I am, perhaps embarrassingly, in a bit of a rush. I am here to see the Dowager Duchess."

"Oh?" Kendal tipped his head back to look up at Edmund. "You know my stepmother?"

"Yes. We were most recently together at Blickton."

"The matchmaking house party." His lips quivered as if he were trying not to laugh. "Tell me, were you aware of its purpose before you went?"

"I was, yes."

"So you went hoping to find a wife?" He narrowed his eyes briefly. "Or perhaps something else?"

"I went with the intention of finding a wife. I am forty and without an heir."

"Past time, then." Kendal nodded. "I suppose I shall come to the same crossroads. I shall be happy to wait another sixteen years."

"Wait however long you must, but take my advice —don't let the one you want get away."

"Spoken like a man who's made that mistake," Kendal said softly. He stood. "Why are you here to see my stepmother?"

"To propose marriage. It is my fervent hope she will

accept. I wanted to speak with you—to obtain your support and blessing if you are inclined to give it. Also to tell you it would be a privilege to count you among my family. You are the most important person in Genie's life, so I would hope that we could establish a relationship. I don't seek to be your father, of course. But I would gladly occupy whatever role you deem acceptable."

Kendal opened his mouth, then closed it again. His brow furrowed. Then he looked toward the painting of his father and Genie. "I miss him very much. I wasn't a very good son the last few years before he died. I disappointed him."

"I don't think so. You frustrated him—at least that was my impression. But he was always exceedingly proud of you."

Kendal snapped his attention back to Edmund. "You knew him well?"

Edmund lifted a shoulder. "Well enough. We worked on committees together in the Lords and occasionally drank together at the club. As I told you when you first took his seat, he guided me when I entered the Lords. He was a good man."

"He was indeed," Kendal said quietly. "As you seem to be. Does my stepmother return your affection? I assume you hold her in high esteem, but you didn't say."

"I love her beyond words." Edmund smiled. "The opportunity to make her my wife is not something I will let slip away—if she'll have me."

"Ironically, you are not the first gentleman to propose marriage to her today. No, not today, I suppose Sterling actually proposed yesterday."

Edmund's heart stopped for a moment. "Sterling is here?"

"Was. He left earlier, as did my stepmother."

Oh God, he was too late. A searing pain tore

through him, stealing his breath. He turned his gaze toward the windows but saw nothing.

"I should clarify," Kendal said. "She turned Sterling down, and he left. She departed a short while after in order to pursue the man she prefers."

Edmund blinked. He looked back to Kendal. "And who is that?"

"She didn't say, and I didn't press her. She did, however, tell me she was going to Staffordshire. That is where your seat is located, is it not?"

"Yes, but I'm not there." It was a ridiculous thing to say, but all he could manage. She'd turned Sterling, with his four children, down! And it seemed she was on her way to him—the man she preferred. There was only one thing to be done, tired as he was. No, not tired. He was suddenly more energized than he'd ever been in his life. "When did she leave?"

"A few hours ago. You could make up the time on horseback, probably, but it will be dark before you catch her. My guess is she will make it to Lancaster for the night."

Edmund nearly laughed. If only he hadn't left the hunting lodge! But how would he have known to find her in nearby Lancaster? "I'll get there."

"You'll need a new horse," Kendal said, moving toward the door. "I have just the one to get you there quickly."

"Thank you."

Kendal stopped in the doorway and turned to face him. "I'd be pleased to count you as family."

Edmund smiled at him, but only nodded in response.

"It is, however, up to my stepmother." He pivoted and continued out of the room.

Yes, it was. Edmund followed quickly, eager to find out.

CHAPTER 11

*T*he rain started just after Genie arrived at the Bell and Whistle in Lancaster. She cursed the sky, then begged it to stop. Wet, muddy roads would add at least a day to her journey. She wanted to get to Edmund *now*.

What if he'd ended up pursuing one of the other women at the party? Perhaps he was even now contemplating marriage to Mrs. Makepeace, or Genie's friend Lettie. No, Lettie would have told her. She'd written recently, and there'd been no mention of Edmund.

Mrs. Makepeace, however, was a distinct possibility. Or another woman who'd been at Blickton. There was no telling what had happened after Genie had left early. Actually, there was, because Cecilia and written to her. There'd been no mention of Edmund matching—or being interested in—anyone.

Genie's stomach growled, reminding her it had been some time since she'd nibbled on something in the coach. Her maid had gone downstairs to check on dinner. Hopefully, she would eat soon. Then sleep, then get back on the road to Edmund.

A knock on the door of her room startled her. Why would her maid not just come in?

Genie rushed to open the door, a question on her lips. "Why—"

The words died on her tongue as she took in the welcome—but quite sodden—form of Edmund.

"Good heavens, Edmund! You're soaked!" She pulled him into the room and steered him toward the fireplace.

"Good evening, Genie. It's good to see you too."

She heard the humor in his voice. "You need to warm up." In reaching for his coat to help him take it off, she froze. There could be only one reason for him to be here, couldn't there? "How did you know I was here?"

He took off his hat and sailed it toward the corner. In its rather damp state, it didn't go very far. His gloves, already removed from his hands, followed the hat.

Edmund shrugged his coat over his shoulders and stripped it away. "As it happens, I have been at Rotherham's hunting lodge the past few days—it's rather near here."

"Oh." So this was a coincidence? She took his wet coat and went to hang it on a hook near the door. Turning, she saw that he'd sat in a chair by the fire and was removing his boots.

"This morning, I rode to Lakemoor. I arrived this afternoon. Unfortunately, you were not there."

Her heart sped as she picked up his boots and stood them near the hearth. "Why did you come?"

Edmund clasped her hand. "You think I need an heir, but I don't really. I have one, and I'll educate him to be the earl."

"But—"

He squeezed her fingers. "I don't need any children of my own, not if it means not having you. I'm hoping Titus won't mind having a stepfather."

Genie's throat constricted. She wasn't sure she could speak. "You want me as I am?"

"Yes. The question is whether you want me, childless as I am."

"I have been a mother and a wife. Anything else—especially you—is a gift I'm not sure I deserve."

He stood and caressed her cheek. "Why would you think that? Everyone deserves love, even a second time." He grazed his thumb along her jawline. "You especially. You've lost so much."

The ache in her chest seared for a brief moment before changing into something bright and beautiful. "I've also gained a great deal. I have a wonderful stepson. I take it he told you where to find me?"

"He surmised you would stop in Lancaster for the night. I am pleased to find he was correct. He said you were on your way to see the gentleman you preferred, or something similar. I am fervently hoping that is me."

She nodded, pressing against him. "It is."

Edmund put his arms around her. "He also told me about Sterling. Poor chap." He shook his head pityingly.

"Do you really feel sorry for him?"

"Not in the slightest. God, Genie, when I think you might have said yes…" He tightened his hold. "Why didn't you?"

She twined her arms around his neck. "Because I love you. Having married for love once, I find I cannot do it again without the same depth of emotion."

"You can't love me the way you loved Jerome," he said quietly, with perhaps a touch of sadness.

Genie cupped the back of his head. "Not the same way, no, but just as fiercely. You're sure about not having a child of your own?"

"*You* are what I need." He looked into her eyes, his

lips curling into a wry smile. "I was a fool not to tell you that at Blickton. Twice a fool, actually. I saw you when I was twenty, and I was instantly smitten. But I was a young buck on my way to travel the continent, and you were the toast of the Season. I didn't think I had a chance of winning you."

"You didn't even try?"

He let out a low, sharp laugh. "I told you I was a fool. Then, when you arrived at the house party, I was overcome with surprise and joy. It was as if Fortune had given me another chance. I should have told you then what I am here to tell you now, that I love you, that I have loved you, that I *will* love you until the end of time."

Genie couldn't breathe. For a moment, she felt as though she was betraying Jerome, to love this man before her as keenly—but differently—as she had him. "Oh, Edmund." She kissed him, pressing her body into his and realizing she was now becoming damp from his wet clothes.

Laughing, she pulled back. "You're getting my dress wet," she said, laughing.

"Then I shall just have to remove it." He lifted his hands to her face and gently held her. "Will you marry me, Genie? I realize becoming a countess is a step down, but—"

"Shh." She put her mouth on his and kissed him soundly. "Now you're being silly."

He smiled against her lips. "Perhaps."

She could hardly believe their fortune at finding each other. "You can truly accept me as I am?"

"I am honored to have you exactly as you are. Just please tell me that I will be enough, that you'll give me the chance to make you happy."

Impossibly, love filled her heart, joining with the love she still held for Jerome, for Titus, for Eliza. "You already have."

EPILOGUE

February 1811, London

Genie reviewed the names on the guest list for her annual start-of-season ball. Old friends, new friends, family—it was the only Society event Titus attended. He'd become reclusive and unapproachable in the years since his father's death. Not to her and Edmund, of course. To them, he was a loving son and still the light of her heart.

"Pondering the guest list?" Edmund asked as he came into the sitting room that adjoined their bedchamber. He brushed a kiss against her temple.

"Just looking to see if any of the eligible young women will catch Titus's eye. It's my only chance to see that he meets *someone*."

Edmund chuckled as he sat down at the table opposite her and picked up the newspaper. "You mustn't pester him too much. He thinks he's on a timetable to match me. Which means he has another nine years in which to find his true love."

Genie looked over at Edmund sharply. "He didn't really say that, did he?"

"Years ago—when I went to Lakemoor to propose to you."

"But I wasn't there." Genie recalled how he'd arrived at the inn in Lancaster, soaked from the rain. "Do you remember when you found me?"

He peered over the paper at her, his eyes narrowing seductively. "Which part?"

"I had to warm you up, if memory serves. It was a terrible sacrifice."

Laughing, he set the paper down. "You didn't seem to mind at the time. Until your maid arrived to announce dinner. That was a trifle awkward."

"She understood. She's still with me, after all."

"That she is."

It wasn't entirely related, but thinking of her maid provoked an idea. "I wondered if I should hire a companion this Season."

Edmund had picked up the paper again, but he didn't read it. His dark eyes fixed on her, one brow arching. "Why would you need a companion when you have me?"

"You detest shopping."

"More than anything." He shuddered. "You shop with your friends."

"Yes, but wouldn't it be nice if I hired a young woman, someone whom I could help find her place in the world?"

Edmund set the paper down and stood. He circled the table and took her hand, turning her in the chair so she could face him while he knelt before her. "My dearest love, if you want to hire a brood of young women, you have my full support. Mothering and caring come naturally to you."

Over the years, they'd discussed adopting a child or two, but they never had. At first, they'd been enthralled with each other. Then they'd had young family members come to stay—Cecilia's children and

Edmund's presumptive heir so he could learn about the estate he would one day inherit.

It never bothered Edmund that he didn't have a son of his own, a fact Genie couldn't entirely understand but for which she was grateful. They'd made a good life and had a wonderfully happy marriage.

"You don't mind?" she asked, referring to the companion she wanted to hire.

"I don't. But," he hesitated briefly before continuing, "if there is something lacking—with our marriage—you'd tell me, wouldn't you?"

She brushed her palm along his jaw, her thumb stroking his cheek. "Of course I would. There is absolutely *nothing* lacking in our marriage. I am full to the brim—with happiness, contentment, and love." She leaned forward and kissed him.

"Your mentioning the night in Lancaster has quite distracted my brain, and now I'm consumed with thoughts of how I might fill you in a more... physical way." He stood and pulled her up from the chair.

Genie laughed deep in her throat. "We just got out of bed a short while ago."

"So?" He put his arms around her and trailed his lips along her throat. She cast her head back to give him more access. "When has that ever stopped us?"

"Never." She clasped his nape and brought his mouth to hers, kissing him wildly.

He pulled back. "Hmm, I do have an appointment soon. Perhaps we should wait."

She dug her fingers into his head. "Edmund, if you leave me now, I will never forgive you. We'll be quick." She flashed him a brazen smile, then tugged him back into their bedchamber. "Just toss up my skirts, and we'll be on our way."

He tugged her back against him as they crossed the threshold. "Have I told you lately how grateful I am to your cousin for inviting you to that house party?"

"It's been some time, but since you send her a gift every year on the anniversary of the occasion, your point has been well made."

"So long as you understand just how much I love you."

She put her mouth near his and whispered, "No more than I love you."

Want to find out what happens when Titus goes to his stepmother's ball and why he's been a recluse? Read **THE FORBIDDEN DUKE**!

Read on for a collection of additional scenes and stories featuring your favorite characters from The Untouchables set during the holidays!

THE FORBIDDEN DUKE
YULETIDE EPILOGUE

Haven't read The Forbidden Duke yet? Grab your copy today and discover how Titus and Nora met and fell in love!

Yuletide 1811
Lakemoor, Lake District, England

"I'm so pleased the weather cooperated with us," Lady Satterfield remarked as she gazed out the window at the clear blue sky. It had rained so much of late, so this was a welcome change. Particularly today.

Eleanor St. John, Duchess of Kendal, flicked a glance toward her mother-in-law before turning from the window. "Yes, I'm so relieved. I'd hate to have to postpone today's activities."

Lady Satterfield pivoted with her. "You're certain Titus has no idea?"

A smile crept over Nora's lips as anticipation welled in her chest. "If he does, he's excellent at concealing it. He specifically said he was looking forward to a cozy day inside. Since the baby started kicking, he enjoys trying to provoke him." Nora caressed her growing belly.

"Or her," Lady Satterfield said, her eyes sparkling.

Nora chuckled. "Or her."

Lord Satterfield entered the drawing room at that moment, rubbing his hands together. "Ah, here you are. Everything's arranged."

Nora nodded. "Titus is in his office with the steward attending to a few things. I will interrupt him shortly."

"Excellent." Lord Satterfield grinned, looking between them. "I admit I'm quite looking forward to this."

"Me too," Nora agreed. "I've never been on a Yule log hunt before."

"Even if you had, I doubt it would compare to this" Lady Satterfield said. "My former husband made sure to include as many of the tenants and retainers as possible." Her gaze glowed with love as she recalled the previous duke who'd died almost a decade ago. She moved toward her current husband and clasped his hand. She'd been lucky enough to find happiness a second time with the Earl of Satterfield.

Lord Satterfield squeezed her hand in return, and Nora felt a lump in her throat. Goodness, strong emotion came so easily since she'd become pregnant.

Nora coughed and blinked lest tears decide to pool in her eyes. "I'm quite excited for the feast afterward." An affinity for food, particularly sweets, was another side effect of carrying the babe. "Keeping the feast planning secret from Titus has been the most difficult piece." They'd enlisted everyone in the household to help with today's surprise for Titus. It was astounding that no one had said anything to him —or at least Nora hoped they hadn't.

She so hoped he liked what they'd planned. He missed his father and had felt guilty for many years about not spending more time with him when he was ill before he died. Nora hoped that this hunt would remind Titus of happier times as well as help him feel as though he could truly carry on his father's legacy. The previous duke had been beloved by his retainers and tenants and Nora wanted the same for Titus. He was very dedicated and worked hard, but he didn't always allow himself to relax and simply *enjoy*. It was a characteristic that had added to his reputation as the Forbidden Duke. He seemed unapproachable and aloof, and for the most part he was content to embody that role. Nora, however, knew a different Titus. Her husband of the past several months was warm and loving, and she wanted everyone to know it.

"I suppose I should go get him." Nora looked expectantly between her in-laws, and they gave her encouraging smiles.

She made her way to Titus's office and knocked softly on the door, which stood ajar.

"Come in," Titus called.

Nora stepped inside as the steward stood from his chair. "I didn't mean to interrupt," she said.

Titus got up from behind his desk and smiled warmly at her. "You're not, we're finished." He nodded at the steward who turned and started toward the door. He exchanged a knowing glance with Nora as he departed.

Nora focused her attention on her handsome husband, and her breath caught, as it often did. They'd married last spring, but her heart still beat wildly when she was with him. She smoothed her skirt over her belly as she moved farther into the office. "I thought we could go for a ride in the barouche today. It's so glorious outside after all this rain."

Titus came around his desk and approached her, his brows pitching down. "I wanted to stay inside and snuggle with my beautiful wife." He slipped his arms around her and nuzzled her neck.

Nora giggled. "We do that every day."

He kissed the flesh beneath her ear, his lips warm and soft. "Is there a limit?"

A sigh escaped her mouth as he trailed his mouth along her jaw. "No. But I really would like to go out while we can. Please?" She pulled her head back forcing him to stop and straighten.

He frowned slightly as he stared down at her. "I'd rather not. Truly. I think we should stay in. Especially in your condition." He patted her belly and turned away from her to return to his desk.

Nora tried not to feel slighted. "That's absurd. I can go for a ride in the barouche."

He shook his head. "It's far too cold."

Frustration grew in her breast. "It isn't. The sun is out, and it's quite fair. Besides, I'll have a blanket."

"I'm afraid I insist we stay inside."

"You *insist*?"

He sat down in his chair. "Yes. Now, if you'll excuse me, I have a few letters I must respond to before we can commence snuggling."

As if she wanted to snuggle with him now. He was ruining everything! "What if I insist on going out?"

He narrowed his eyes at her. "I'll give strict instructions that the vehicles are not to be taken out."

Nora resisted the urge to stamp her foot. Or throw something at his stubborn head. "You're being beastly. I just want to go for a simple ride." And restore a long-held tradition. As well as create a memory they'd cherish forever. It was their first Yuletide season together after all. It was also Nora's first away from her sister, a fact she tried not to think about. Today's festivities would help with that.

Titus leaned back in his chair and looked up at her. "It's not simple. The ground is saturated. It would be too easy for the barouche to get stuck in the mud. Why don't you read for a bit, and I'll join you shortly in the drawing room?" He gave her a bland smile before looking down at his work.

Having been dismissed, Nora stared at his dark head and scowled. She spun on her heel and stalked back to the drawing room where the Satterfields were expectantly waiting. Their faces fell in unison when they saw her.

"What's wrong?" Lady Satterfield asked, rising from the settee.

"He refuses to go. He spouted some nonsense about my condition and mud." Nora folded her arms over her chest. "Now what do we do?"

Lord Satterfield, who'd stood with the countess, exhaled. "I'll talk to him. You both get ready, and we'll meet you in the entry hall." He gave them both a look of pure determination before leaving.

"Do you really think he'll succeed where I failed?" Nora asked, dropping her arms to her sides.

Lady Satterfield patted her arm. "I hope so dear. Otherwise, we've gone to a lot of trouble for nothing, and many people will be greatly disappointed."

Nora prayed that wouldn't happen.

～

Titus frowned at the door after Nora had left. He *was* a beast. He wouldn't have hesitated to take Nora for a ride, but it was imperative they stay at home today. He would move heaven and earth to give his wife her heart's desire, which was precisely why he wouldn't take her out in the barouche.

He winced as he recalled the disappointment in her gaze followed by shock and then anger. He hadn't meant to patronize her and hoped she'd forgive him.

Of course she would. Later today, she'd be too happy to remain upset.

Or so he hoped.

His stepfather walked into his office, his face dark and his mouth turned down. "Why won't you take Nora for a ride? It's absolutely beautiful, and she's been cooped up inside for days."

Titus stood up. "I just don't want to go out today. I'll take her out tomorrow."

Satterfield, a typically affable fellow, gave him a hard look. "And what if the rain returns? There's absolutely no reason you can't go today."

There was every reason, but he wasn't going to explain himself to his stepfather. "This is my house, and I'll decide what reasons are valid." Titus inwardly flinched —that didn't sound good or rational even to his ears.

"Would it help to know that your wife has planned a special outing for today and by not going, you'll be crushing her?"

Hell. A special outing? What was he supposed to do now? *He'd* planned something special for today, and they could *not* leave.

Titus walked around his desk as he pushed out a breath. "I didn't realize. Still, we can't go today. Can't we just do this tomorrow?"

"Certainly. If you'd like to sleep alone for the foreseeable future. You're still a newlywed. You don't understand a woman's anger. It is a force unto itself."

Titus wiped his hand over his brow. "I'm not trying to make her angry." Damn it all, this was not going as planned.

"We never *try*, son. Nevertheless, that's precisely what you're doing."

There had to be some sort of middle ground, but Titus couldn't think of it. "I'm sorry, but we just can't go today."

Satterfield glared at him a moment, and Titus wasn't sure he'd ever seen him that put out. "Then we'll go without you. You really are the Forbidden Duke, aren't you? You forbid yourself even the simplest pleasures. Enjoy your solitude." He turned and strode from the office.

Titus gaped after him. He did like his solitude, but since he'd fallen in love with Nora, he far preferred her company. And actually the company of others he cared for. Including his stepfather.

He followed Satterfield all the way to the entry hall and stopped short. The butler began to help the earl into his great coat while Titus's stepmother and Nora pulled on their gloves. "You're going anyway?" Titus asked.

The bitter taste of defeat rushed over his tongue. He'd planned today's surprise for Nora so meticulously. The rain had tried to ruin things, but after several delays, it was finally going to happen—Nora's fondest Christmas wish.

Only she wouldn't be here to receive it.

Realizing this had moved past his ability to control, Titus surrendered. "How long will this excursion take?" Perhaps if they hurried, they would still arrive home in time.

Nora gave him a cool stare. "All day. Don't let us disturb you."

"I'll go," he said somewhat listlessly.

His stepmother pursed her lips at him. "We don't want to force you."

He didn't say anything, just waited for a footman to fetch his greatcoat and hat.

A few minutes later he joined them outside where the barouche was already waiting. He blinked toward the bright sky. It *was* an especially fine day. Perfect for a surprise.

Ah well, it would still be a surprise, just not the way he'd conceived it.

He climbed into the barouche and sat beside his wife who refused to look his way.

This was not how he'd envisioned this day at all.

∾

Nora slid a curious glance toward her husband. He looked incredibly disappointed. He really didn't want to go out today. And here she was forcing this on him. How much fun were they going to have *now*?

She opened her mouth to tell him what they had planned when the sound of a coach drew her attention. The barouche slowed as the coach came toward them.

The other vehicle eased to a stop beside them in the drive. Nora's heart stuttered. She recognized that coach.

The door flew open, and her beloved sister, Joanna, popped her head out as the footman rushed to put down the stairs.

"Nora!" Jo cried, her hazel eyes sparkling in the sunlight.

The tears Nora had kept at bay earlier welled in her eyes she stood up in the barouche. "Jo, you're here." She could hardly believe it.

The footman opened the door to the barouche and helped Nora down. As soon as her feet hit the earth, she rushed forward and wrapped her sister in a tight hug. Tears tracked down her cheeks, which were pulled taut with the smile that came from her very soul.

When they finally parted, Nora could see that Jo was crying too. "I was certain we wouldn't be together." Nora wiped her eyes.

"I was too, until your husband invited me to come." Jo looked over Nora's shoulder at Titus.

Nora turned her head and saw Titus watching them with a wide grin. "This is why you didn't want to leave." How she loved this man.

He nodded.

Lady Satterfield dashed her fingertips over her eyes. "Well, this is just the loveliest surprise."

Yes, it was. Or was it? They still had one to go. Nora hugged her sister again and whispered, "Come in the barouche with us, I have a surprise for Titus as well."

Jo's eyes glinted with mischief. "You two are inspiring." She sighed, and Nora detected a bit of envy. Belatedly, she looked toward the coach.

"Your husband isn't with you?" Nora asked.

Jo shook her head. "No, he didn't wish to leave the vicarage." She didn't sound disappointed in the slightest. There would be time to talk about *that*. Hopefully she'd be staying for a nice long visit.

"Come," Nora said, turning.

The footman helped them both into the barouche and soon they were on their way again.

With the addition of Jo, Nora was pushed up against her husband, but there was nowhere she'd rather be. "Thank you," she murmured. "I understand why you were being awful before."

He chuckled softly. "I hated every moment of it."

She beamed up at him. "I love you so very much."

He pressed a kiss to her forehead. "And I adore you."

She hoped he still did in a few minutes.

They left the drive and made their way toward the village before veering onto a track that led to one of Titus's tenant's houses. She tensed and held her breath as she watched for his reaction.

Dozens of people were clustered about, and their voices rose with cheer as the barouche approached.

"What is this?" Titus breathed.

"We're going on a Yule log hunt," Nora said, hoping he would be as happy as he'd made her.

His gaze was fixed on all of the tenants gathered together. His steward stood in the front, grinning. "My father used to have those," Titus said.

Nora clutched his arm and gave him a loving squeeze. "I know. Everyone was thrilled to have another. It was long overdue, they said."

He opened his mouth, but nothing came out. He snapped it shut and nodded. A moment later he turned toward her, the shine of unshed tears in his lush green eyes. "Thank you."

"Happy Christmas, my love."

He kissed her again. "Happy Christmas."

THE MAGIC OF MISTLETOE

The middle part of this story is the prologue of The Duke of Kisses. Haven't read it yet? Grab your copy today! To read how the characters in this story met and fell in love, don't miss The Duke of Daring, The Duke of Deception, and The Duke of Desire!

December 1817
Suffolk, England

Ivy, Duchess of Clare, collapsed onto the bed, her face flushed and tears leaking from her eyes. She wiped her mouth and let out a soft groan.

"Here," Lucy, Ivy's friend, the Countess of Dartford, said as she set a cool cloth on Ivy's brow. "Aquilla's fetching a glass of water."

Aquilla, the Countess of Sutton, joined Lucy, a tumbler of water clasped in her hand.

Ivy blinked up at her two closest friends and managed a weak smile. "I'm so glad you're here. I'm just sorry I'm sick. This is supposed to be a festive, happy time."

One of Lucy's dark brows arched high on her forehead. "Are you sure it's not? When was the last time you had your courses?"

Ivy's jaw dropped for a moment. She hadn't even considered... "I don't know. Leah isn't even six months old yet. I haven't bled since she was born."

Lucy and Aquilla exchanged a pointed look.

"Have either of you?" Ivy asked, feeling slightly panicked. She wasn't sure she was ready to have another child—if, in fact, that was what was happening.

Both women, who'd had their first children in April, nodded. "Just last month for me," Aquilla said.

Lucy snorted. "Apparently I was 'lucky.' My courses returned by August."

"You've always been the lucky one," Aquilla said cheerfully, causing them all to giggle.

Ivy's stomach tilted again, but she didn't think she had anything left to vacate. "Help me sit up so I can drink that water."

Lucy scrambled to prop her up and Aquilla handed her the glass. The cool liquid slid down Ivy's throat and settled into her belly without any fuss, thank goodness. Her hand strayed to that spot, where only recently she'd carried Leah.

Ivy sent a glance toward the cradle at the foot of the bed where her daughter lay sleeping. Miraculously, Ivy's sudden illness hadn't awakened the baby, but then the majority of her retching had occurred downstairs in the drawing room into a nearly century-old Wedgwood vase, which one of the maids was now carefully cleaning.

"Better?" Aquilla asked with a hopeful tilt to her mouth.

"Yes, thank you." Ivy settled back against the pillows as her husband, West, ducked into the chamber.

"All right?" he asked, concern darkening his brow.

"Good enough," Ivy responded.

"We'll see you downstairs when you're recovered," Lucy said, inclining her head toward Aquilla and then the door.

With a nod, Aquilla followed her out.

Sebastian Westgate, Duke of Clare, the notorious Duke of Desire sat on the edge of the bed next to Ivy and fingered a coppery curl back at her temple. "The vase came clean, you'll be happy to know."

"Oh, good." Ivy had been horrified, but it had been the nearest thing and she hadn't hesitated when Lucy had scooped it up and handed it to Ivy as she began to convulse with the need to empty her stomach. "I'm sorry to ruin the tree decorating."

Even though the children were all still babies, they'd decided to erect a tree, making a celebration of it by inviting their dearest friends who'd arrived just yesterday.

"You've ruined nothing, my love." He leaned over and kissed her forehead. "I'm just glad you're feeling better. Did you eat something that didn't agree with you?"

Ivy chewed the inside of her cheek, uncertain if she should reveal her suspicions—rather her friends' suspicions. She wasn't entirely sure she believed it. She hadn't been ill like that when she'd been carrying Leah. Ultimately, she decided to make light of it and see what he said. "Lucy suggested I might be with child again. But it's far too soon."

West's reaction started with a flash of surprise followed by a hint of doubt and then unadulterated joy as a smile spread his lips. "I should be thrilled if that were the case." He sobered, adopting a concentrated expression and a formal tone. "Let me see."

He lifted his hand to her breast and cupped her through the layers of clothing. His touch was firm but gentle and when his thumb flicked over the tip, Ivy sucked in a deep breath, her earlier sickness completely forgotten in a flare of lust.

It seemed they both came to the same conclusion at the same time.

"I'm with child," Ivy said.

"You're with child," West said.

They both laughed, and it was a moment before Ivy asked, "How do you know?"

"Your breasts have a very distinctive feel when you're carrying. It shouldn't surprise you to hear that I know *precisely* what that feels like."

No, it didn't, given how fond he was of touching her there at every opportunity. Indeed, his hand still lingered against her, reminding her of the need pulsing between her legs.

"And how did you know?" he asked mildly, his thumb making another pass across her breast.

"As you know, I was particularly...insatiable. Indeed, if you don't lift my skirts right this instant, I'll be forced to throw you onto the bed and have my way with you."

His brows darted up his forehead for a scant moment before settling low over his darkly seductive eyes. "I can't decide which I prefer." The words were a purr, rustling over her as provocatively as the incessant stroke of his thumb.

In the end, they opted for a combination of both, as Ivy lifted her skirts and climbed atop her husband, careful to be quiet lest they wake the baby, for one *never* woke a sleeping baby.

～

"The tree is beautiful," Aquilla said as she stood back from the massive evergreen and surveyed their decorating progress. Fruit and sweets hung from the branches along with a collection of glass baubles. The candles would go on last, but Aquilla had to admit she wondered if the entire thing might catch on fire. She supposed it could if they weren't careful. They'd just be careful.

"Not as pretty as you," Ned, her husband, said softly as he came up behind her and slipped his arms around her waist. He drew her back against him and sprinkled feather-light kisses against her neck.

A delightful shiver raced down Aquilla's spine. "You're biased."

"I'm not. Everyone agrees the Countess of Sutton is one of the loveliest women in all of England. But they're wrong. You're *the* loveliest."

Aquilla smiled, and a soft sigh escaped her lips as Ned's tongue teased the sensitive spot beneath her ear. "Peregrine will be up from his nap soon."

"Then perhaps we should take advantage of our free time..." His teeth caught her earlobe, arousing another shiver.

Aquilla turned in his arms, murmuring, "Perhaps," as she stood on her toes to press her mouth to his.

They were, unfortunately, interrupted by the arrival of Lucy and her husband Andrew, the Earl of Dartford. Lucy held their son Alexander who was just eight days older than her and Ned's son, Peregrine.

"Uh oh, we're interrupting," Lucy said.

Andrew laughed. "It's a drawing room, not a bedchamber. They know where to go if they want privacy."

Ned let out a frustrated snort but grinned nonetheless. Aquilla fixated on her godson and held her arms out. "Come see Auntie Aquilla!"

Lucy delivered her son to Aquilla who snuggled the boy close and dropped a kiss on his dark head. He lifted his rich, earth brown eyes to hers and smiled as he recognized her. "Gah!" he said in greeting.

Aquilla wrinkled her nose at him. "Gah yourself. I can't get over how big he and Peregrine are already," she said to Lucy. "Just think, next year they'll be running around and pulling things off the tree."

"Perhaps we ought to forego a tree," Ned said. They'd already offered to host next year's festivities. Since they'd spent last year together at Darent Hall—Andrew and Lucy's house—and this year here at Stour's Edge, it seemed they had a tradition and next it would be their turn.

Aquilla playfully smacked her husband's bicep. "Nonsense. We are *having* a tree."

"Don't bother arguing with them once they've made up their mind," Andrew said. "On second thought, don't bother arguing with them *ever*."

Ned nodded in agreement while Aquilla looked down at Alex and said, "Your father is a smart man."

West and Ivy came in at that moment, their daughter Leah snuggled in her father's arms. Her hazel eyes lit when they saw Alex. Upon seeing her, he squirmed in Aquilla's arms. "Do you want to play with your friend?" she asked.

Ivy fetched a blanket and laid it on the floor. West sat Leah down and Aquilla set Alex in front of her. Lucy set down a pair of silver rattles, which Alex and Leah were soon waving about. Their nonsense words and laughs filled the room with the sound of the rattling silver.

A moment later Ivy glanced about before asking, "Does anyone know where Fanny is?"

Fanny was Ivy's younger sister. Just twenty, she'd come to live with Ivy after Leah was born and would have her first Season in the new year.

"I haven't seen her since she went for her walk," West said, frowning.

That would have been hours ago. Though Aquilla had only been here a few days, she already knew the household routine and Fanny went for a walk each morning.

Ivy looked outside where fat snowflakes fluttered to the already-white ground. "It's been snowing for over an hour." Her face creased with concern. "If only I hadn't been ill and..." She scowled at West who sat beside her on one of the settees. "I should've noticed she wasn't home."

West clasped her knee. "She'll be fine, I'm sure. Sometimes she gets distracted, particularly if there's an animal involved."

"That's my concern. What if something happened? What if she's trapped in the snow?" Ivy stood, her concern blooming into stark worry. "It will be dark in a few hours."

West got to his feet beside his wife and stroked her back. "Don't work yourself into a dither. It isn't good for the baby."

"That's true," Andrew said. "Alex hates it when Lucy's agitated."

"Not that baby," Aquilla said before realizing she perhaps not to have said that out loud. "Oh!" She clapped a hand over her mouth and sent Ivy and apologetic look.

"It seems I am with child again," Ivy said without releasing a bit of her stress. "But I'm fine—or I *will* be fine once Fanny is home safe."

"Then let us go and fetch her," West said before pressing a kiss to Ivy's temple. "Come lads." He motioned for Andrew and Ned to join him, which they did with alacrity.

"I'll be back soon," Ned murmured. He kissed Aquilla quickly before departing.

"I'll never forgive myself if something happens to her," Ivy said.

Lucy went to her friend and rested a comforting hand on her shoulder. "They'll find her."

"Maybe I should go with them." She started toward the door, but Lucy tightened her hold and Ivy swung her an irritated stare.

Lucy narrowed her eyes. Of the three of them, she

was the most likely to impose her will—and be successful. "You'll do no such thing. You need food after this morning's events, and you need to rest. We insist." She looked over at Aquilla who nodded in agreement.

"I'll ring for tea and we'll wait." *And pray,* Aquilla silently added.

∼

Fanny glared at the rabbit hole but quickly acknowledged she was angry with herself, not the tiny animal she'd foolishly followed through the copse and up the hill and over an icy stream.

Blast, she was an idiot. She'd seen the rabbit hunkered down near a tree. It had seemed to be shivering, and so she'd decided to scoop it up and take it home before it succumbed to the elements. But as soon as she'd moved close, the animal had scampered away.

Satisfied the rabbit would be fine, Fanny watched it run until it stopped. Then it sat down and began to quiver again. That had started what seemed to be a game of cat and mouse as Fanny went after it, and it ran away then stopped again. Over and over until it had disappeared down its hole.

"Well, I suppose I did see you safely home," Fanny muttered. "You're welcome!"

She pulled her woolen cloak more tightly about her and looked up at the muted sky as the first snowflake struck her square on the nose.

"Oh, to be that snowflake," a masculine voice rent the quiet, drawing Fanny to spin about toward the source of the sound.

A tall gentleman lounged against a tree as if he frequented hills in the middle of a snowstorm with careless ease. Er, possible snowstorm. Fanny squinted her eyes toward the heavens once more and wondered just how far from Stour's Edge she'd strayed.

"Miss?"

There was that voice again, reminding her that the snow and her unknown location were perhaps not her most troubling problems at present.

"I'm on my way home—to Stour's Edge," she added hastily.

A single dark brow arced into an upside down V as he pushed away from the tree and sauntered toward her. "I see. You must be the Duke's bride."

"I am not."

The man's dove-gray eyes flickered with appreciation as his gaze slid over her. "I see. How nice."

Was he flirting with her? Fanny had next to no experience with that. Mr. Duckworth had tried such nonsense with her, but his efforts always seemed far more...lascivious. She would forever thank her sister from saving her from certain doom. Without Ivy inviting her to come live at Stour's Edge, Fanny would have undoubtedly found herself the next Mrs. Duckworth. The third, in fact.

Best to just let this gentleman know she wasn't the sort of woman he might think. "I'm afraid I'm not adept at flirting, nor do I have any interest."

"Was I flirting?" He moved closer. "I didn't intend. But I never do, and then a beautiful woman happens across my path and I simply can't help myself." His lips curved into an arresting smile.

Fanny's breath caught. He was the most handsome person she'd ever clapped eyes on. And he was looking at her as if he maybe thought the same thing about her.

Except, he'd just said he flirts with all beautiful

women, which meant this wasn't a singular event for him, as it was for her. And really, she wasn't beautiful. Far from it. She had freckles and her lips were too full, as her mother was fond of pointing out. "You're definitely flirting," she said warily.

"And you are on your guard. As you should be. You're a bit far from Stour's Edge, however. Are you certain that is where you are from?"

He doubted her? Actually, perhaps it was best that he did. This was a scandalous encounter, and it would behoove her to keep it from becoming known. Which meant she couldn't tell anyone about it, and she didn't want *him* telling anyone about it either.

"I think I'll just be on my way." She turned from him and started down the hill. She made it about twenty feet before she stopped and frowned. She had absolutely no idea where she was going. *Blast it all.*

"Are you lost?"

The question came from far too close behind her, and she jumped. She quickly turned and backed up at the same time, moving quickly and without care for her location near the top of the hill. Just enough snow had accumulated that she slipped.

And tumbled down the hill.

She landed in a heap at the bottom, her eyes closed and her body smarting from rolling over a few times on the way down.

"Hellfire!"

The proximity of his deep voice made her open her eyes. The concerned, yet still unbelievably handsome, face of the stranger hovered over hers.

"Are you all right?" he demanded, his gaze darkening to the color of iron.

Fanny moved her fingers and toes. "I think so." Her backside stung most of all, and she was acutely aware of the frigid temperature of the ground beneath her. "It's quite cold down here."

He knelt beside her, but quickly clasped her waist and pulled her to stand, rising to his feet in front of her. "Better?"

And now she was acutely aware of his hands on her and the delicious, almost entirely foreign sensation of being held.

She quite liked it.

"Yes," she said rather breathlessly, realizing she sounded like a ninnyhammer and not caring in the slightest.

"I insist on seeing you home." He looked up at the sky as the snow seemed to be falling in larger flakes than it had just five minutes before. "Where is that?"

She was cold and now wet, and for some reason she felt safe with him. "Stour's Edge."

He gave a firm nod then wrapped her arm over his. "We'll walk briskly. If you can."

She nodded then wiped at the dirt and grass that seemed to cover her cloak. He helped her, his hand moving over her hip and then her backside. The moment he made that contact, their gazes connected.

"Sorry," he murmured before averting his gaze.

They walked in silence for a few minutes, a hundred questions tumbling through her head and an equal amount of sensations coursing through her body.

He glanced over at her, a snowflake landing on his dark lashes and melting almost immediately. "I know we haven't been properly introduced, but it seems we should take care of that."

"It's a bit scandalous, isn't it?"

"No more so than my caressing your backside."

Caressing. Oh dear. Those hundred sensations doubled.

"I'm Frances." She decided it was best to just keep things simple. He didn't need to know she was Fanny Snowden, sister-in-law to the Duke of Clare.

"I'm David."

"Pleased to meet you David." For all she knew he was a footman at a neighboring estate. She doubted that, however. While her experience with anyone outside her tiny village of Pickering in Yorkshire and its environs was limited, she could tell he was Quality. Or at least good at mimicking it.

"What brought you so far from home?" David asked.

"Providence, thankfully." She realized belatedly he didn't mean *that* home. She blamed the fact that she'd just been thinking of Pickering. Though she'd been at Stour's Edge for nigh on six months, apparently she could still think of her lifelong home as home.

He gave a soft laugh. "Because you met me?"

Now she realized how that may have sounded. "No, I didn't mean that. I meant... Oh, never mind. I am abysmal at polite conversation. I've almost no experience with it."

"Are you in service?" he asked, voicing about her what she'd just been thinking of him.

She seized on the opportunity to mask her true identity and have a way to explain why he couldn't escort her to the house. "Yes, I'm a maid." She looked at him askance. "What about you?"

"In service?" He started to shake his head but then stopped. "Not precisely. I'm serving as apprentice to a steward."

"That sounds exciting."

He turned his head toward her. "Indeed?"

"Oh yes. To be responsible for so many things... You must be quite intelligent."

He shrugged. "My father always told me so."

"My father always told me I was a featherbrain."

"I find that hard to believe." He said this with utmost certainty. "Although, you did wander far from home in a snowstorm."

"It wasn't snowing then, and I was trying to save a rabbit." She exhaled. "I'm afraid I'm terribly soft-hearted when it comes to animals. My father also told me I was far too kind. Once, he made me abandon a litter of puppies after their mother died."

David gasped. "That's atrocious."

She nodded, glad for his support. "Yes, but I sneaked back out to where they were and rescued them anyway. One of the neighbors had a dog who was almost finished nursing her pups, and she was more than glad to adopt the four little babies. Ironically my father took one of those dogs several months later, never realizing it was one he'd left for dead." She shook her head. "He loved that dog more than any of us, I think."

"What an astounding tale. I would say you have a kind heart, not soft. There's a difference, I think."

She swung her gaze to his. "Do you?"

"I do."

They stared at each other a moment before she tried to trip over a rock. He caught her, his free hand clasping her hand while he gripped her arm. "All right?"

"I'm also rather clumsy."

"Then allow me to assist you over the stream, though I gather you made it across by yourself earlier."

They'd arrived at the slender, but swift-moving brook. "It was a miracle, really."

He laughed then withdrew his arm from hers. "I'll go first and help you." He leapt over the water with ease, and she decided she could watch him do that a thousand times. In her mind's eye, she would.

He held his hand out to her. "Ready?"

She clasped his appendage, and he brought her over the stream with a fluid grace she didn't possess on her own. "I bet you're a fine dancer," she said.

He grimaced. "Barely passable, I'm afraid."

"I'm quite good. That is one area in which I seem to possess adequate agility."

He chuckled. "A maid who dances and rescues animals. You are a treasure, Frances."

Heat rose in her face, but she suspected her cheeks were red from the cold and was relieved he couldn't see her blush.

He tucked her arm over his once more and they started on their way, keeping up their rapid pace. "Do you often get lost?" he asked.

Only when she struck off in a new direction and then only sometimes. Snowstorms were particularly helpful if one wanted to lose their way. "No, but then I just left home for the first time less than six months ago." She wished she hadn't revealed that much. But he was so easy to talk to.

"You're new to your employment then?"

"Yes. What about you?" she asked, hoping to divert the conversation away from herself lest she bore him with the story of her life. "What are you doing out in the middle of a snowstorm?"

"I'm afraid I was just taking a walk. Then I saw you running up the hill, and I was curious."

"So you followed me?"

"Guilty." But the look he cast in her direction didn't reflect even a tinge of regret.

She was glad and more than a little...tantalized. "Well, I suppose I must be grateful since without your help I would be lost and cold."

"But dry. I can't imagine you would have fallen without my intervention." Now she detected a dash of remorse.

"That's a nice theory," she said wryly, "but I did tell you I was clumsy."

"I suppose we'll never know," he mused. "Come, let's move a bit faster or we'll both be soaked to the skin."

She had a sudden vision of him in clothing that was plastered to his muscular, athletic frame. Muscular? Yes, she could tell from his arm and the way he'd lifted her effortlessly from the ground and assisted her across the stream. Athletic? Evidently given how quickly he'd made it down the hill after she'd fallen and the fact that he hadn't lost his balance as she had. Besides all of that, she had eyes, and she could see he was broad-shouldered and long-legged.

"Do you often go for walks?" she asked, thinking he must.

"Every day. At least once. Like you, I have an affinity for animals. In my case it's birds."

"Indeed? What are your favorites?"

"It's very hard to say," his response was solemn, as if he were deeply considering her question. "I find myself drawn to birds of the marsh—it's their long legs and long beaks, I think. There's something very graceful about their composition and demeanor. Avocets are beautiful. As are godwits."

"I know next to nothing about birds." But she suddenly wished to correct that and planned to scour West's library for every book on ornithology she could find.

"I could teach you," he offered softly.

It was the nicest, sweetest, most alluring offer she'd ever received.

Too bad she couldn't accept. He was a steward's apprentice, and she was the sister-in-law of a duke destined for a grand Season and probably a marriage to a prince. Or at least a duke. That was what she and Ivy joked about at least.

Ivy! She had to be worried sick.

"How far are we from Stour's Edge?" Fanny asked.

"About a quarter mile, I should think." He pointed

in front of them. "There." You'd see it if not for the copse of trees and this damned thickening storm.

She recognized the copse from earlier and from the walks she'd taken since coming to Stour's Edge. It was the stream that had taken her off course—she hadn't yet crossed it, probably because it had been much wider during the summer months after she'd first arrived.

When they reached the trees, she stopped. "We should part here, I think."

"You probably don't want to be seen arriving with me," he guessed accurately.

"I don't think that would be wise. I've been gone too long as it is."

"Are you sure you can find your way?" he asked.

She nodded. "Yes, I'm quite oriented now. I meant it when I said I didn't usually get lost."

"But what about the dancing?" He moved slightly closer. "How am I to know if you can truly dance?"

"If we meet again, I'll show you," she promised, even though she knew that would likely never happen.

"I'll hold you to that." He glanced up at the sky, blinking. "It really is snowing hard. You should go."

"I should."

And yet neither of them moved. They stood there facing each other, arms still clasped, cloaked in white, seemingly alone in the world.

"Pity there isn't mistletoe," he said softly.

Oh, he wanted to kiss her!

Good, she wanted him to kiss her too.

She edged closer until they almost touched, chest to chest. "Let's pretend there is."

He pitched his head toward hers, and she closed her eyes just before his lips touched hers. They were cold but soft. His arms came around her, and he held her close.

The kiss continued, awakening all of her senses and arousing them so that to her mind there was just him and her and the snowy quiet enveloping their secret embrace. When his tongue licked along her lips, she opened for him, driven by curiosity and a sweet hunger she'd never experienced.

Once inside, his tongue met hers, and he coaxed her fully, showing her what it meant to really be kissed. She'd always wondered, and now she knew.

It was over far too soon, and the cold that he'd banished from her for a few, brief minutes came rushing back, reminding her that she was cold and damp and needed to get inside.

He brushed his gloved fingertips along her cheek. "I refuse to say good-bye, so I'll just say, Happy Christmas."

She refused to say good-bye too, even though she knew it was. "Happy Christmas."

Then, before she could lose her courage, she turned and fled.

By the time she reached the door to the drawing room at the rear of the house, she was breathless, both from her dash through the snow and her encounter with David.

Ivy met her at the door, her forehead creased. "Fanny! I've been so worried." She pulled her sister inside and wrapped her in a fierce hug." When she drew back, she looked down at Fanny's snow-covered cloak. "You're soaking wet."

"And now you are too," Fanny said with a touch of irony.

"So it would seem." Ivy raised her gaze to Fanny's. "Where have you been?"

"Trying to save a rabbit."

"Of course you were," Ivy muttered. "West and Dart and Ned are out looking for you, silly. I'll send some footmen out after them. In the meantime, go upstairs and take a warm bath."

"Yes, Ivy." Fanny leaned forward and kissed her sister's cheek before departing the drawing room. On the way, she waved at Lucy and Aquilla who were on the floor with the babies.

Later, when she was warm and dry, Fanny joined everyone for dinner. She apologized to West and the others for having to go out in the snow looking for her. They were all just glad she was all right.

Afterward, they placed small candles in the tree and when they were lit, Fanny gasped with wonder.

Ivy, holding her nearly-asleep daughter against her chest, moved close to Fanny's side, smiling. "It's beautiful, isn't it?"

"It is."

"Who knows where you'll be this time next year," Ivy said with a touch of sadness. "You may be married. I'll miss you, especially when we've just found each other." Ivy had left home more than a decade ago and had only renewed contact with Fanny and the rest of their family last fall.

"I'll miss you too. I may not be married. Maybe I'm meant to be a spinster."

Ivy laughed. "No, not you."

"You nearly were."

"Yes, and as you can see, you can never be too sure about the path you're meant to take."

Fanny thought about the path she'd taken that day and wished it had ended differently.

West came over then and slipped his arm around Ivy. "Oh look, Dart is hanging some mistletoe."

A feeling of warmth coupled with a pang of loss wrapped around Fanny's heart. She knew right then that she'd never look at mistletoe the same.

Or Christmas.

~

The house was quiet when West climbed into bed next to his wife. Gathering Ivy close, he kissed her forehead, her cheek, her delicious lips. She sighed as she snuggled into his chest.

"Tonight was beautiful," she said.

"Right up until we had to extinguish every one of those candles." That had taken great care so as not to catch the entire bloody house on fire.

Ivy laughed. "Don't you think it was worth it? I don't care—we're doing it every year. Just imagine Leah's face next Christmas."

"And her little brother's." He brought his hand around to his wife's belly and stroked the soft plane through the linen of her nightgown.

"Oh, you think this one will be a boy?" Ivy asked.

"I was right about Leah, wasn't I?"

"Yes." Ivy traced her fingertip around his chest, arousing him with the simplest touch. "Did Fanny seem different to you tonight? She was quiet."

"She was." Fanny liked to talk and talk, but tonight she'd seemed a bit distracted. "I expect she was tired after traipsing after that rabbit she never caught."

"Yes, that must be it. I'm so glad she's here with us." Ivy rolled West to his back and rose over him, her eyes darkening with desire. "Have I thanked you for welcoming her into our family?"

"Many times, but I shall always accept your appreciation."

"What about my undying devotion?" Ivy reached down and stroked his rapidly-hardening shaft.

"I'll take that too." He let out a soft groan as her hand worked its magic. "You're going to drive me mad, woman."

She grinned down at him. "But you'll enjoy it, won't you?"

"Every blessed moment." He clasped the back of her neck and brought her mouth to his for a soul-searing kiss. "Happy Christmas, wife."

"Happy Christmas, husband."

THE DUKE OF RUIN
CHRISTMAS SCENE

This is a "deleted" scene from The Duke of Ruin. Simon and Diana were recently married at Gretna Green and are on their way back to his estate in the south of England. They are traveling over Christmas and stop in Oxford for a few days to celebrate the holiday. Enjoy! If you haven't read The Duke of Ruin, grab your copy now!

December 24, 1817

"It's Christmas Eve!" Simon Hastings, Duke of Romsey leapt from the bed with excitement. And then promptly dove back under the covers where it was far warmer next to his new wife.

"Too cold?" Diana asked, smiling as he burrowed against her.

"Hell yes, what was I thinking?"

"That it's Christmas Eve morning?" she offered helpfully.

He kissed her soundly and pulled her against him. "Our first one together. We have much to do. Did I mention I told Mr. Margrave that I'd help him bring in the greenery to decorate?"

"No, you did not." She wriggled her body, shifting

his arms so that they were face to face. "I thought we were going to take a walk to look at the spires and then watch the mummers?"

"All that too."

She arched a single dark brow at him. "Do you ever rest?"

"Occasionally when I'm in bed. But only occasionally. And not when I have a beautiful woman in my arms." He ducked his head and licked her neck then suckled her flesh.

"Simon! Last time you did that, you left a mark. Since that was just yesterday, it's still there."

Yes, he *had* done that. And it had been delightful. He kissed down her collarbone. "I do think I may be late to meet Mr. Margrave."

"Pity," she said, not sounding the least bit sorry.

He wasn't late, however, because he wasn't helping Mr. Margrave. After leaving Diana in their room, Simon stole from the inn and made his way down the lane. He'd found a goldsmith the day after they'd arrived and had commissioned him to fashion a wedding ring for Diana. The hammered iron band he'd bought her at Gretna Green was pretty, but temporary. His duchess should have gold and jewels. In fact, her ring would be a sapphire.

Simon entered the small establishment with a spring in his step.

The proprietor, a young man of small stature with large, round spectacles, looked up and immediately blanched. "Good morning, Your Grace."

"Good morning," Simon said a bit warily. "I trust you have my wife's ring ready?"

Still pale, the proprietor, Mr. Abernathy, now winced. Then he burst into tears. Simon couldn't help but feel sorry for the man.

Abernathy wiped his eyes and took a deep breath. "I'm so sorry, Your Grace. I'm afraid I've lost it."

"*Lost* it?" Simon repeated.

"I stayed the night with my sister and her family last night—my brother-in-law has been ill. I was still working on the ring, so I took it with me to finish." Abernathy wrung his hands together, sniffing. "Somewhere on the way to the shop this morning, it fell through a hole in my pocket. I retraced my steps a dozen times, but I wasn't able to find it."

Disappointment spun through Simon's gut. "It isn't your fault."

"Oh, but it is, sir. Now you don't have a gift for your duchess." He started to cry again then abruptly turned and disappeared into the back of the shop behind a curtain. When he emerged, he held out a small pouch. "Here is your deposit."

Simon accepted the money with a slight nod, his mind working as to what he could give Diana instead. He'd been so looking forward to slipping that ring on her finger tonight.

"I added a little extra," Abernathy said. "For your trouble. And for my mistake."

Simon eyed the man and could see that his coat was rather worn. He believed there could be a hole— or two—in the garment. "You needn't give me extra. It was an accident. I am sorry you are out the commission."

The man nodded but said nothing. He looked as if he might be holding his breath. Or trying not to cry.

Bloody hell.

Simon thrust the pouch back at him. "Take it."

Abernathy's dark eyes widened behind the glass of his spectacles. "I can't—"

"Of course you can. Happy Christmas." He offered the man a smile and left the shop.

As he made his way back to the inn, he wondered what he was going to give Diana now.

⌒

Diana accompanied the innkeeper's wife, Mrs. Margrave, and her two daughters as they distributed breads and cakes they'd baked to some of the people in their neighborhood. To a person, they were in need, whether due to age or illness or something else. Diana was glad to help and only wished she'd had something to give.

Their next to last visit was a family of five—the Browns. The father had been ill, but finally seemed to be on the mend. The wife was delighted to have two loaves of fresh bread, and the two smaller children were thrilled to have Shrewsbury cakes. The father thanked Mrs. Margrave profusely for her generosity. The oldest child, a boy who was maybe ten, didn't take a cake until his younger sisters had each had two. He kept his head down and made fleeting eye contact with Diana who smiled at him warmly.

As she and the Margraves made their exit, Diana thought about the people they'd visited and wondered if she and Simon could help them somehow. She had nothing—she couldn't even buy Simon a gift. Would he want to help? There were so many things she didn't know about her new husband. And yet she felt certain he possessed a kind and generous nature.

They arrived at their final destination, which was a particularly small abode so Diana volunteered to remain outside. Mrs. Margrave assured her they would only be a moment.

"Your Grace?"

Diana started at the small voice that came from behind her. She turned to see the boy from the last house. "Where did you come from?"

He ducked his head shyly. "I came to ask you something, if I may."

"Of course." She squatted down to his level. "How can I help?"

He reached into his pocket and pulled out a piece of jewelry—Diana caught a flash of gold. "I have this ring. It...belonged to my grandmother. I wondered if you might want to buy it from me. My father hasn't worked in over a month, and this would help us have food." His cheeks flushed brilliant red, and he couldn't meet her eyes.

Diana's heart clenched. She might not have any money, but Simon did, and he would certainly help. "You are a kind and brave lad. Let me see it."

He opened his hand to reveal a gold ring with a brilliant sapphire.

"Oh, it's beautiful," she said. It seemed a very expensive piece for a family of their means, but how could she know their circumstances? "It belonged to your grandmother?"

He looked at her and nodded profusely. "It did, ma'am."

"Are you certain your parents wish to part with it?"

He looked away again. "Yes, ma'am."

Diana worried he was perhaps not telling the truth. What if his parents had no idea he'd taken it?

She took his hand and curled his fingers around the ring. "You keep this for now, all right? I will come around in a while to buy it from you. What is your name?" She would talk to Simon about what to do. At the very least, they needed to give the family whatever they might need. It broke her heart to see this boy resort to selling family heirlooms.

He nodded again. "Owen, ma'am. Thank you. I'll be waiting for you outside."

She wanted to tell him not to, for it was cold, but suspected he didn't want his family to know what he was about. She felt rather certain his parents didn't know he'd taken the ring. To feel so desperate... Diana had suffered many dark times in her past, but they didn't compare to this.

The Margraves came from the house, and Owen dashed off.

❧

Simon paced the common room of the inn, which was now festooned with enough greenery to resemble a forest. He was no closer to coming up with a replacement gift for Diana.

She came inside just then with Mrs. Margrave and her daughters. Garbed in a puce walking dress, her cheeks pink from being outside in the cold, she was absolutely ravishing and he was incapable of doing anything but stare.

Gliding toward him, her forehead creased. "Oh, Simon, you must help me."

Worry clenched his gut, and he took her hand. "What's happened?"

"Nothing to me, but I've met a family we must help. I hope you won't mind. I have no money of my own." She winced, and he stroked the back of her hand.

"My funds are now yours," he said, smiling. "Tell me about this family." He led her to the settee near the front window, and they sat down.

"They live around the corner. Mr. Brown has been ill for some time, and they don't have enough to eat. Mrs. Margrave took them bread and cakes, and I suspect those will be the finest things on their table for Christmas."

Simon frowned. "That's a shame. Shall we take them supper?"

"Yes, please. I'd also like to give them money to help them while Mr. Brown continues his recovery."

Simon leaned forward and brushed his lips against hers. "You have the kindest heart. Of course we will help them."

She smiled and curled her arms around his neck in a tight hug. "Thank you, Simon."

He stroked her back and would have continued the embrace had they not been in the common room of an inn. Instead, he pulled back with great reluctance.

They sought the Margraves' help in assembling a supper for the family, which had included a visit to some of the market stalls. Simon had joked that it was their walk to see the spires of Oxford University, which were of course visible just about anywhere in town.

Carrying the food they'd gathered, they made their way toward the family's home.

"Thank you for doing this," Diana said. "I felt so bad for this family's plight. They have three children. The oldest is a boy—Owen—who can't be more than ten. He tried to sell me his grandmother's sapphire ring, but I'm certain his parents didn't even know he'd taken it. The poor dear."

Simon's ears pricked at the word sapphire, and his mind worked through what she said. "A sapphire ring?"

She nodded. "It looked quite valuable. I hope you don't mind, but I don't want to buy it from him. They should keep their family heirloom."

They approached a series of houses, and a small boy loitered near the end of them.

"There he is," Diana said.

They went to the boy, and Diana introduced them. "Owen, this is my husband, the Duke of Romsey."

Owen bowed and did not raise his eyes.

Simon tried to give the boy a warm smile of encouragement, but it was difficult since the lad wouldn't look up. So Simon sank down. "Owen, I understand you have a ring to sell me."

Diana nudged him with her leg, but he didn't turn his head to her.

"I do, Your Grace." He put his hand in his pocket and withdrew the ring that had been meant for Diana —Simon recognized the sapphire and puzzled the pieces together.

"Is your uncle a jeweler?" Simon asked softly.

The boy's gaze lifted then, and there was surprise as well as a bit of fear. "Yes."

Simon nodded. "Well, I would be delighted to buy your ring. How much do you want?"

Owen chewed his lip then gave Simon a dubious look. "Two pounds?"

"That is far too little for such a valuable piece. Here, take this." Simon reached into his pocket and pulled out a good deal more than the boy had asked for. Simon picked up the ring and held it between his thumb and forefinger. "Are you certain you can part with this?"

"I am, Your Grace."

"Very well." Simon put the money into the boy's hand and rose.

Owen's eyes widened with wonder and his cheeks turned bright pink. "Thank you. God bless you, Your Grace." He bowed to Diana. "And you, Your Grace."

"We have this for you, too." Diana handed him her packages, and Simon handed him what he'd been carrying. "It's Christmas Eve supper. Or Christmas Day."

"Thank you, Your Grace." Owen blinked rapidly.

Diana smiled at him. "Take care, Owen."

Simon clutched the ring in his hand, and put his arm around Diana as they watched the boy run to his door and disappear inside.

"That was very generous of you," she said softly. "But you shouldn't have taken the ring. It belongs to their family."

He turned to face her. "No, it belongs to you. I commissioned it from his uncle who lost it this morning."

Diana's eyes widened, and her mouth opened. She lifted her hand to her lips. "Owen stole it? He seemed like such a sweet boy."

"I'm sure he is," Simon said. "The ring fell from the jeweler's pocket. I suspect Owen found it and saw an opportunity to provide for his family. I must say, I can't fault him for that."

"Still, he should have returned it to his uncle."

"Yes, but all's well that end's well. Isn't that how the saying goes?"

She nodded. "Shakespeare."

"Your Grace?"

Simon turned, along with Diana, toward the voice. It was the jeweler. "Mr. Abernathy, allow me to present my wife, the Duchess of Romsey. Diana, this is the man who made your ring." He held it out to Abernathy, who gasped in surprise. "Would you believe I found the ring just here a moment ago?"

"It's a Christmas miracle!" Abernathy crowed in delight.

"It is indeed," Simon said.

The jeweler turned to Diana. "I hope you like it, Your Grace."

"It's beautiful. Thank you very much. Are you on your way home?"

Abernathy blushed. "I'm going to my sister's house."

Simon reached into his pocket. "Now that I've found the ring, I must compensate you for it, Mr. Abernathy."

Holding up his hand, Abernathy shook his head. "You already have, sir."

"Nonsense. That was just a deposit.

"Let the difference be my gift to you, for your kind understanding when I thought it was gone."

Simon pressed the money into his hand, knowing it would go to good use for this man and his sister's family. "I insist. Happy Christmas, Mr. Abernathy."

The man beamed. "Happy Christmas, Your Grace!"

Simon offered his arm to Diana and they started back toward the inn.

"Let me understand," she said. "You paid Mr. Abernathy even though he'd lost the ring?"

"Yes."

"And you bought a ring from Owen that you'd already paid for—at least partially?"

"Yes."

"Then you didn't tell Mr. Abernathy that his nephew had taken the ring and tried to profit from it?"

"Heavens no."

She stopped and turned, putting her gloved hand against his cheek. "I have nothing to give you on this Christmas Eve, while you have this lovely ring and your amazing generosity."

"You gave me the greatest gift of all, Diana. You've given me hope for a future I never would have imagined. Not after all that's happened." He pushed the familiar pain of loss away and clung to this joyous moment, to this woman standing before him.

"Happy Christmas, Simon."

"Happy Christmas, Diana. Shall we pretend there's mistletoe?"

She curled her hand around his nape and stood on her toes. "Yes, let's."

THE YULE LOG HUNT

This story features characters from The Duke of Desire, The Duke of Danger, The Duke of Kisses, and Never Have I Ever with a Duke. If you haven't read them, click on the title to grab your copy now!

Christmas Eve 1822
Stour's Edge, Suffolk, England

Part One

Sebastian Westgate, Duke of Clare, was outnumbered. How had he managed to be left alone with five children, only two of whom were his? "Don't you have nurses?" he mused aloud.

"Papa, they are busy," his daughter Leah, all of five and a half years, said with far more authority than she ought to have. "With the other children."

Yes, the younger ones. "What about their mothers?"

Before Leah could answer, three small boys aged three and four began to wrestle in the middle of the floor. She turned her head, pursing her lips in a way that brought her mother to West's mind, and charged toward the melee. "Stop that!"

None of them listened to her, so she raised her voice and tried again. When one of the boys yelled, "Ow!" West resigned himself to intervene. He tried to take a step but realized there was a small body clinging to his leg.

Wee Jasper Kinsley, Earl of Wethersfield and heir to the Duke of Halstead, stared up at West with wide green eyes. "Up, please?" When West didn't immediately sweep him into his arms, Jasper added, "I wanta see."

Ah, the lad wanted to watch the tussle. West couldn't blame him for that. He plucked the boy up and carried him closer to the tangle of bodies thrashing about on the floor. "Better?" West asked.

Jasper nodded. Leah had continued to admonish the wrestling boys, telling them they would be in grave trouble when their mothers arrived. It wasn't lost on West that mothers were the greater threat. He was nothing more than a soft-hearted jelly when it came to his three children, and it was to his wife, Ivy, that they listened. Which was for the best because West could think of no one worth listening to more, no one who could care for them—or him—better.

"What on earth is going on here?" Ivy's voice carried through the room like a captain addressing her troops. She carried their youngest, Julia, who was not yet two.

"Benedict!" Emmaline Maitland, Marchioness of Axbridge, barked at the wrestling boys. The one with the bright blond hair extricated himself—or tried to, but Sebastian, West's son, grabbed his ankle and pulled him back down.

"Sebastian, stop that!" Ivy said crisply. Sebastian promptly let Benedict go and blinked up at his mother. He and the remaining boy, Gray, which was short for Graham for he was named after his father's best friend, the Duke of Halstead, ceased their sport, and all three scrambled to their feet.

Gray swept his hair from his forehead and cast a worried glance toward his mother, Fanny, who was also Ivy's younger sister.

Fanny narrowed her eyes at her son. "Apologize to Aunt Ivy and Uncle West for causing a ruckus in their house."

Emmaline inclined her head toward her son. "You too, Benedict."

"Sorry," they chimed in unison.

"Sebastian, apologize to your mother," West said.

"Sorry, Mama." Sebastian went to take his mother's hand, and West saw the precise moment when his wife melted on the inside. Her green eyes took on that warm, maternal sheen that never failed to make his heart feel as if it might burst. That he'd found a love so strong and so pure would humble him until his dying breath and likely beyond.

"Why is everyone apologizing?" Lionel, Marquess of Axbridge and one of West's closest friends, asked as he entered the drawing room. He carried their youngest, Caroline, who was the same age as Julia and was followed by West's brother-in-law, David Langley, Earl of St. Ives whose arms were full with his youngest, Mary.

"The boys were wrestling," Emmaline explained to her husband.

"Who was winning?" Lionel asked, and West couldn't help but laugh. But then all the women either frowned or glared at him and Lionel, and they quickly sobered.

"What happened?" Fanny asked.

"There was only Papa here," Leah answered, as if that response perfectly summed up why a fracas would break out. And West supposed it did.

"I shouldn't have been left alone with them," he said in meager self-defense.

Leah came to him and touched his hand. "It's all right, Papa. I was here to help."

West stifled a smile and caressed her cheek. "Thank goodness for that." He winked at her then transferred his attention to the other adults. "Are we ready for the Yule log hunt?"

This provoked a chorus of excitement from the children, followed by laughter from the adults.

"I think that's a yes," Lionel said with a wry grin.

Graham and Arabella Kinsley, Duke and Duchess of Halstead, entered then. Graham carried their youngest, Charlotte, who was just a year old. "Did we hear that it's time to leave for the hunt?"

Jasper wriggled in West's arms as he reached for his mother. Arabella strode toward them and embraced him with a smile. "Thank you for watching Jasper while we tended to Charlotte. The nurses are ready to take charge of the small ones while we go on the hunt."

As if on cue, three nurses entered the drawing room and went about taking the smallest of the children.

"Should we bring Mary?" David asked his wife, Fanny. "Or is she still too young?"

"We're bringing Julia," West said. She and Mary were only a month apart in age.

"I would, but she's practically falling asleep," Fanny said. "Next year." She transferred the toddler to the nurse.

Everyone set to bundling up the children and themselves. West indicated the others should precede them outside while he and his family brought up the rear. There were two carts to convey them to the forest, plus a third that would transport the log back to the house.

"You really couldn't keep them from wrestling?" Ivy murmured. She carried Julia while West shepherded Leah and Sebastian toward the waiting cart.

"They're children," West said. "They move too quickly. And there was Jasper. Hell, there were far too many of them. It was me against a rabid army." He caught the slight upturning of his wife's lush mouth.

"Yes, three and four-year-olds are so treacherous. I daresay you're lucky to have escaped unscathed." She slid him a sarcastic glance, a single red-gold brow arching high on her forehead.

"Indeed." He flashed her a grin before lifting their children into the cart. Once they were all settled, the grooms driving the carts set them in motion.

"I wish it was snowing," Leah said wistfully, her head cast back as she looked up at the gray sky.

"That would make our hunt a bit more difficult," Ivy said, stroking Leah's back.

"I suppose." Leah didn't sound convinced.

They dipped through a large rut, and Emmaline, who was seated across the cart from West and Ivy, winced. She clasped her round belly.

"Everything all right?" Ivy asked with concern. "Perhaps you should have stayed at the house?"

"Nonsense. The babe won't come for another month. I wouldn't have missed this." She glanced toward her two children, her features softening. "Or them."

West understood. The joy he once gleaned from finding the Yule log was nothing compared to the joy of watching his children go on the hunt. This was Julia's first, and it would be no less thrilling than Leah's or Sebastian's.

"Perhaps Ivy's right," Lionel said, watching Emmaline with a puckered brow. "Should you really be out here in the cold jostling about?"

"I'm going to *jostle* home before Epiphany. Both Benedict and Caroline were past when we expected them. I can't imagine this babe will be any different."

Lionel's features relaxed in a half-smile, and he leaned over to kiss his wife's brow. "Forgive me if I worry. I can't help myself where you're concerned."

The children chattered nonstop as they rode to the forest. By the time they reached the wood, the energy in the cart was high enough to set a town ablaze, or so it seemed to West. He eagerly helped them all down, where they joined the children from the other cart.

"Now, everyone knows to stay together, right?" West announced.

"They're not listening," Ivy said, gazing over the raucous group. "Children!"

Their conversation dried up like a stream in late summer as they pivoted to face her.

"A captain indeed," West murmured.

Ivy snapped her gaze to his. "What?"

"Nothing." He cleared his throat and addressed the children. "You are to stay together. No one wanders off alone. Understand?"

Most of them nodded.

Ivy shook her head. "Not good enough. We need a roll call. When Fanny says your name, say, 'I understand'."

Fanny began calling out the children's names, and each one dutifully responded. West leaned close to Ivy and whispered, "You are an inspiring force."

She looked at him askance, her eyes sparkling. "Don't you mean terrifying?"

"In the best possible way." He kissed her cheek and lightly squeezed her waist. Suddenly, he was overcome with thoughts of her pressed against a tree in the forest, the Yule log hunt be damned.

"Can we go look now, Papa?" Leah asked, her gaze fairly teeming with excitement.

West grinned at her enthusiasm. "Yes, go find us the best Yule log!"

The children instantly scattered, and the adults called out to each other to follow them in various directions. West and Ivy stuck close to Julia since she was so small. She wasn't looking at the trees at all. She was simply trying to keep up with her big brother Sebastian as he raced off in search of the perfect log.

"This one, Papa!" Sebastian called.

"No, that's not nearly big enough," Leah said. She looked about and pointed at another tree. "That one is better."

"Is not," Sebastian argued, his lips forming a pout. He stalked in the opposite direction while Leah marched toward the tree she'd indicated.

Julia followed Sebastian, and West was torn as to which way to go. Ivy was already going after Sebastian and Julia, so West turned to trail behind Leah. Except she was with several of the others, so he opted to stay with his wife, lest she end up having to tend Julia.

"Look, Mama, toadstools!" Sebastian declared as he squatted down next to a cluster of woodland fungus.

"We look but never touch, dear," Ivy said to him with a smile.

Julia squatted down next to him and reached her hand out, but Sebastian gently took it in his. "No, Julia, don't touch." He looked around then guided her to a moss-covered rock. "Touch this instead. It's soft." He removed his mitten and showed her. He then helped her to take off her mitten so she could feel it. Her giggle filled the air and warmed West's heart.

"If someone had told me I could love someone

more than you..." He shook his head as he glanced toward Ivy. "I would have said they were mad."

"And I would have said the same." She moved close to his side, sliding her arm around his waist. "But the way I love you is quite different than the way I love them." She narrowed her eyes slightly as she pressed against him.

He turned, taking her in his arms. "I should hope so." His lips descended on hers, and their kiss ignited his desire.

"Disgusting!"

West and Ivy pulled apart, laughing at their son's horrified outburst.

"West!" David called from several yards away.

Ivy went to take Julia's hand. "Come, let us see what Uncle David wants."

Instead, Julia held up her arms. Ivy lifted her and settled the toddler on her hip.

West clasped his son's hand. "Do you suppose they found a tree?"

"But I want to pick the log, Papa."

"We must all agree on one." West began to question the wisdom in bringing eight children into the forest and expecting them to agree on the same Yule log. It had been hard enough before the children. Everyone had their own opinion on what constituted the perfect log.

They joined the others who stood around a fairly sizeable tree.

"It's too big," Fanny said, her mouth tipped into a slight frown.

"Is not," Benedict said.

Gray nodded in agreement. "This one."

"Yes, this one," Sebastian said.

"This seems almost unanimous," David said. "At least among the older children. I daresay the others won't care." He grinned.

"What does Leah say?" West asked, looking about for his daughter, who was the oldest child. When he didn't immediately see her, he called out her name.

"Oh!" Emmaline's knees buckled, and her eyes rounded.

Lionel rushed to her side, catching her before she fell to the ground. He swept her into his arms as if she were a feather and not a woman far along with child. "You're going back to the house."

"I think that's best." She winced. "My waters have broken."

Lionel swore softly as he hurried to the cart. West followed him. "I'll go with you."

"West!" His name came as a panicked plea from his wife. "Leah isn't here."

West spun about as ice plucked at his heart.

"Neither is Jasper." This dark pronouncement came from the boy's father, Graham.

Lionel settled Emmaline into the cart and handed her a blanket before turning to West. "Stay. I'll take Emmaline back."

Fear tripped along West's spine, but he tamped it down. Leah and Jasper couldn't have gone far. But Emmaline and Lionel needed to return to the house immediately.

"We'll go too and take the children so you can focus on finding Leah and Jasper," Fanny said, nodding toward her husband, who set to gathering them. He and Lionel began loading them into the second cart. Emmaline let out a gasp and gritted her teeth.

"Go," David said to Lionel. "We'll be right behind you."

Lionel thanked him, then climbed into the cart with his wife. The groom steered the horses back toward the house.

Julia began to cry as Ivy handed her to Fanny. "Don't cry, love," Ivy said softly, patting Julia's back.

"Aunt Fanny will be with you, and I'll be home before you know it." She smiled warmly, but West saw the unease in her eyes.

West picked up Sebastian and set him in the cart. "Look after your sister."

"You'll find Leah?" The boy's dark eyes were wide with worry. "She can pick whatever log she likes."

"Don't worry, we'll find her in a trice," West said as much to alleviate his own concern as his son's. He kissed the boy's forehead and told the groom to drive.

When he turned, Ivy, Graham, and Arabella were already striding through the trees calling for Leah and Jasper.

But with each call that went unanswered and each minute that passed, West felt as if he'd swallowed lead. His unease became fear, and soon his fear would become panic. If anything happened to them, he didn't know what he would do. His gaze strayed to the pale face of his wife, and he refused to give in to dread.

West reached for her hand and squeezed her tightly. "We'll find them."

She looked at him with determination, the steel in her eyes tempered by an edge of alarm. "We have to."

~

Ivy tried to use logic to banish the panic that threatened. She would have expected Sebastian to be the one to run off and not answer when called, not Leah. That fact made Ivy wonder if she'd done so because of Jasper. Or if something terrible had happened...

No. She refused to think such a thing.

Had Leah followed Jasper to keep an eye on him? Though she was only five and a half, she had the natural instinct of a caregiver, probably because she had two younger siblings.

"Jasper!" The agitated sound of Arabella's voice drove Ivy to the younger woman.

Ivy touched her arm soothingly, despite her own apprehension. "We'll find him."

"We should have left him at the house with Charlotte." Arabella looked positively ashen. Even her lips were a faint gray. "I think I'm going to be ill." She turned and rushed away, but the distinct sound of her tossing up her accounts was unmistakable.

Graham hurried to her side and caressed her back. Ivy couldn't hear what was said, if anything.

West pressed his lips together in a grim line. "We'll cover more ground if we split up, but Arabella shouldn't be left alone. You and she must stay together—and stick close to this area in case Leah and Jasper find their way back to the cart. I will strike out with Graham and our men. We'll choose directions and go individually."

Ivy nodded. "A sound plan."

West called out to the groom and four footmen who remained.

She watched as he went to share the scheme with Graham. After Arabella had straightened and Graham had briefly embraced her, Ivy made her way in their direction.

"I want to go search for them," Arabella said, her arms wrapped around her middle.

"We can look around here." Ivy noted that Arabella still looked rather pale. "But perhaps you should sit in the cart for a few minutes and warm up beneath a blanket."

"I'm not unwell. At least, not in a sickness way. I'm with child. I've been meaning to ask you how you manage with three."

"Not very well, apparently," Ivy said. No, she

wouldn't think like that. "Come, we must keep a positive outlook. Jasper and Leah are fine. They've simply wandered off. Perhaps my daughter has taken after her Aunt Fanny and decided to follow a rabbit."

"Isn't that how Fanny met David?" Arabella asked.

Ivy nodded. "You've heard the story?"

"Yes. If not for that rabbit, I would likely be married to David instead." Because their fathers had been best friends and arranged for their children to wed. Unfortunately for their fathers' plans, David fell in love with Fanny. And as luck would have it, Arabella was meant to be with Graham, who had, incidentally, been David's secretary before inheriting a dukedom —much to Graham's shock. David and Graham remained close, which is how Ivy and West had come to know them so well.

"Now here you are expecting your third child with Graham," Ivy said, seizing on a happy thought. "How lovely. As to your question about three children, I have it on good authority that anything after three makes no difference whatsoever."

"Whose authority is that?" Arabella asked, half-smiling.

"Nora, of course. And her sister. Jo and Bran just welcomed their fourth some months ago."

Arabella nodded in recognition. She was well acquainted with both Nora, the Duchess of Kendal, and Jo, the Countess of Knighton. Their circle of friends was quite large when Ivy thought about it. She could never have guessed this would be her life—a duchess, a husband who adored her and who she adored in return, a large group of close friends, family really, who took care of one another, and of course, her children who she loved beyond measure. Her heart squeezed as she thought of her firstborn.

No, not her firstborn. She'd delivered a stillborn child many years ago, long before she'd met West.

When she'd been young and foolish. Before she'd understood what true love really was, what it could be.

"I'm feeling a bit better, I think," Arabella said, drawing Ivy from her thoughts of the past. She walked a few yards. "Jasper! Leah!"

Ivy pivoted and strode in the opposite direction, circling around the cart. "Jasper! Leah!"

They continued calling and walking, widening their range with each pass. Ivy tried to calculate how long they'd been gone, but it was impossible. It felt like an eternity, but it was probably not long at all.

At last, they heard a distant sound. "Arabella!"

Ivy and Arabella froze then turned toward the sound. Arabella started in that direction, and Ivy followed.

"Arabella!" This time was louder.

"It sounds like Graham."

"And it sounds like he's getting closer. Is that a happy tone?" Ivy asked.

"I...think so?"

Then they came into view. Graham carried his son while one of the footmen bore Leah. Ivy and Arabella reached for each other at precisely the same moment, providing the other with the support they needed as a wave of great relief washed over them. At least Ivy assumed that's how Arabella felt. They smiled at each other before breaking apart and rushing to meet their children.

"My goodness, Jasper, you're all wet." Arabella held her arms out, but Graham shook his head and said he'd take him to the cart.

"Mama, I saw a pretty bird. But it flew away."

"That's when he fell into the stream," Leah said. "I had to wade in and help him up."

Ivy took her daughter from the footman. "Thank you, Harris. So much." She surveyed Leah's skirts and feet. She was wet, but not completely so as Jasper was.

"We need to get Jasper back to the house," Graham said. "It's too cold for him to remain out here."

Arabella climbed into the cart. "Give him to me, and I'll wrap him in a blanket." They'd kept blankets from the other two carts for the return trip.

Graham helped wrap Jasper up and settle him in his mother's lap. Arabella fussed over him, but the fear that had tightened her features had gone.

"You didn't see West?" Ivy asked as she set Leah into the cart. She didn't want to leave without him, and yet Jasper had to get inside and out of those wet clothes right away, as did Leah.

"No," Graham said. "Do you mind if we go and send a cart back for him?"

"I'll stay," the footman offered then looked to Graham. "If you don't mind driving the cart, Your Grace?"

"Boyd can drive!" West called, trotting into the clearing with the groom.

Ivy exhaled with relief, though they were still missing the other footmen.

West came to the cart and embraced Leah. "I hope you had an excellent adventure. You gave us a bit of a scare."

"I'm sorry, Papa. I had to keep an eye on Jasper." She cast him a somewhat disgruntled look, and Ivy had to stifle a laugh. "He moves rather fast for a toddler."

"That's my boy," Graham said. He looked to West. "We need to get Jasper back. He fell into the stream and is soaking wet."

"Leah is also a bit damp in the feet," Ivy said.

West surveyed their daughter. "I can see that." He turned to Graham. "Yes, you must go at once. I'll stay and find the others, then we'll chop down that cursed log." He gestured toward the tree the boys had agreed upon.

"Why is it cursed, Papa?" Leah asked. "I like it."

He smiled at her and went to kiss her forehead. "It isn't, sweetling, especially since you like it. Go on home with your mother, and I'll be there soon."

"But then you'll be alone," Leah said, frowning.

West shook his head and stroked Leah's cheek. Watching them together brought another tide of relief and love over Ivy. "I won't be alone at all," West said. "I have Harris and the others to keep me company until the cart returns. In the meantime, we have to cut down our log."

"Can't Mama stay with you? I promise I'll go home with Arabella and Graham, and I'll go straight upstairs for a bath."

Was she really only five and a half? She sounded so mature, but then that's what Ivy had come to expect from her darling girl.

Arabella looked a bit restless. "I'll make sure she does."

Ivy didn't want to debate it—not when Arabella needed to get her son home. "All right then. I'll see you shortly." She gave Arabella a grateful smile. "Thank you."

Before the cart left, Harris removed the axe. He turned to West as the vehicle drove away. "Do you wish to do the honors, Your Grace?"

West looked toward the cart. "I probably should. Leah is watching, and I don't wish to disappoint her." He took the axe from Harris and went to the tree. The other footmen arrived and were glad to hear the children had been found.

"On second thought, I'm going to let you younger men do the hard work lest I hurt myself." West handed the axe back to Harris. "Plus, I need to comfort Her Grace now that the crisis has passed." He winked at Ivy, and the footmen chuckled in response.

Ivy shook her head as her beloved husband came toward her. "You don't give yourself enough credit. You forget that you chop firewood all the time."

"How do you know that?"

"As if you aren't aware that I watch you." She rolled her eyes then settled them on him with a warm intensity. "How can I not when you remove your shirt?"

"I don't do that *every* time."

"No, and that's a shame."

West wrapped his arms around her waist and drew her close to his chest. "You're all right? About Leah, I mean."

"Yes, we'll talk with her about it when we get home. She should have told us she was going after Jasper."

"Except, if she was merely following him, she may not have realized she needed to say anything." He rested his forehead against Ivy's. "Sometimes we forget she's only five."

"And a half. But yes, you're right." Ivy's chest constricted for a moment. "I won't forget that again." She raised her hands between them and grasped the lapels of his coat. "Arabella said she's expecting their third child. She asked if it was difficult to manage three. After today, I can unequivocally say, *yes*."

"Oh dear, does that mean there won't be a fourth?"

"It won't be for our lack of trying."

West brushed his lips against hers. "No, it won't. And I look forward to another attempt later."

Ivy giggled. "Just one?"

His eyes sparked with desire and love. "Oh, now you're tempting me. But then you always do, my love. Don't ever stop."

"Never." She kissed him, heedless of the footmen and their task, even when they felled the tree.

It was a Yule log hunt she would never forget.

~

Part Two

Lionel cringed as the cart hit another deep rut in the track on the way back to Stour's Edge, West's ancestral pile. Emmaline let out a low moan and squirmed on the seat.

"We're almost there," he said encouragingly.

She pushed out a long breath and narrowed her eyes at him. "We aren't either. I need to get off this bench. Will you help me to the floor of the cart?"

"Anything." He just wanted her to be comfortable and safe. And for their child to be safe.

Picking up an extra blanket, he spread it on the wood floor of the cart. He guided her from the bench and eased her onto the blanket. She took the blanket that was already draped around her and settled it across her midsection. "Would you sit behind me so I can lean on you?" she asked.

Lionel moved quickly to position himself so she could be more comfortable. He put his legs on either side of her so she was nestled firmly into his embrace and could recline against his chest. Then he pulled the blanket up to her neck. "How's this?"

"As good as it's going to get, I'm afraid." The last word ended on a sharp intake of air.

He felt her body tighten and knew a pain was shooting through her. He recalled the births of their first two children all too well. "Just breathe, my love." He slid his hands beneath the blanket and gently massaged her biceps.

The pain seemed to last longer than any of the

others, which he knew was not a good sign. Well, it was a good sign as far as the babe coming soon, but he wanted to make sure they got back to Stour's Edge and had time to organize everything for the birth. He still couldn't believe it was already happening. He turned his head and urged the groom to drive faster.

When the pain subsided, she melted against him, her body feeling like jelly. Lionel kissed her temple.

"Why is this babe coming early?" Emmaline ran her hands over her belly in large, circular strokes.

He heard the worry in her voice and worked to keep any from his. "She's impatient. Clearly, she saw how much fun we were having on the Yule log hunt and wanted to join in."

"She? You always assume I'm having a girl."

"And so far I've been right fifty percent of the time. I like my odds."

"The hunt was fun until Leah and Jasper went missing. I hope they've been found."

"I'm sure they have," Lionel said, bringing his hands to her shoulders and then sliding them back down to her elbows.

Her body clenched again, and Lionel held his breath. He looked toward the manor house, willing it to come into sight. *Come on.*

The cart hit another rut, the deepest one yet. Lionel and Emmaline flew up off the floor and crashed back hard. Emmaline cried out as the cart pitched. The rear corner dove toward the earth, and it was obvious to Lionel that they'd lost a wheel.

"Bloody hell!" He held tightly to his wife as the pain worked through her. He turned his head and watched as the groom leapt from the front seat and dashed around to the back of the cart.

The groom's gaze met Lionel's, and it was all Lionel needed to see. He looked again in the direction of Stour's Edge. They were at least a mile away. How could he carry a laboring woman that far? He could do it—he *would* do it. But she'd be in agony.

"The other cart will be along shortly," the groom said.

Emmaline relaxed in his arms. It was due to the pain subsiding, Lionel knew, but he was sure the groom's proclamation helped.

Lionel couldn't believe he hadn't thought of the other cart. A great relief rushed over him. "Of course. We'll just wait. I'll hold on to you, my love."

"I feel as if we're sliding toward the ground," Emmaline said.

He realized it was more than just a feeling. They were slipping in the direction of the lost wheel. He looked to the groom. "Will you help me remove her from the cart?"

The groom nodded and sprang to action. He reached for Emmaline's hand. Once he had her in his grip, he used his other hand to brace her upper arm and shoulder. Lionel pushed back from her and slid around her other side. Keeping hold of her, he guided her down the cart then scrambled from the vehicle. Once he was on the ground, he bent and picked her up. The groom let her go, and Lionel hefted her in his arms.

"Grab the blanket and spread it on the ground," he bade the groom.

The groom took the blanket and settled it off the track near a tree. Lionel set Emmaline down so she could lean against the trunk. "The other cart will be here shortly."

She grimaced as her belly tightened once more. "We're out of time."

"No, we're only a mile from the house. We'll get there before the babe comes."

Her gaze met his. "Lionel, you aren't understanding me. The babe is coming now."

He blinked at her. "She can't."

She tipped her head to the side, her eyes nearly closing until they were mere slits. "I've done this before. I think I know when my babe is about to be born."

Of course she did. As much as he wanted his child born under a roof, he knew that children did whatever they damn well pleased.

"What do you want me to do?" Fear and anxiety gripped him so hard he could barely breathe.

"The blanket, please." She had to work to get the words out as she endured a lasting pain. Lines grooved into her forehead, and her lips paled.

Lionel grabbed it from where it had fallen when he'd swept her into his arms. "What do I do with it?"

"Bunch it... up." She exhaled long and loud. "Put it behind me."

The bark had to be hard against her back. Blast, he should have realized that. He did his best to make a giant pillow of sorts then leaned her forward to place it behind her. Gently, he guided her backward so that she was propped up.

She readjusted her position, moving her backside down and parting her legs as she planted her feet on the ground. "You're going to have to guide him out."

He noted that she referred to the babe as a he but decided this was not the time to engage in an argument. Dropping to his knees, he lifted the hems of her skirts, pushing them up to her knees. Right away, he saw the top of the babe's head. He'd seen this before, but there'd been a doctor present! And Emmaline had been inside! On a bed!

Lionel swallowed and eased forward so he was between her calves. He steeled himself for what would come next. There would be liquid and yelling and, he prayed, a babe's cry.

"I need a hand!" Emmaline growled.

"I'm helping," Lionel said.

She pulled her skirts back until her thighs were completely exposed.

"To hold!" she yelled.

Lionel looked at the groom, who'd stood back and frankly looked as if he wanted to disappear into the ground. "Come hold her hand, please." Silently, he pleaded with the man to swallow his discomfort and be a source of help and comfort.

Thankfully, the groom hastened to Emmaline's side. He was careful to avert his gaze from her exposed lower half as he took her hand. Emmaline instantly squeezed it so hard his fingers turned white.

"Sorry about that," Lionel murmured, knowing from experience how fierce his wife's grip was.

Emmaline cried out and bore down, her face turning red. Liquid rushed from her as the babe's head came free. Lionel clasped the warm, wet scalp as emotion barreled into his throat. He held it back. Later he would give in, but now he needed to focus completely.

"The head is free," he said.

There was a moment of respite as Emmaline drew deep breaths, and the groom's hand regained its flow of blood. Then she groaned as she pushed again, this time freeing the babe's shoulders.

The sound of the next cart brought welcome relief, but Lionel didn't take his eyes from his child. He held onto her slick body gently but securely.

"Oh my god! Everyone stay in the cart." It was Fanny. "David, fetch a blanket for the babe."

Lionel glanced up at Emmaline's face and saw the relief in her gaze just before she tightened once more, her body bearing down as she pushed the child from her body.

Clasping the small babe, Lionel stared at the perfect form, red and wrinkled, and very much what he'd predicted: a girl. She did not cry. Instead, her blue eyes were wide as they took in the world around her. She looked as amazed as he felt to have welcomed her to the world beneath a tree along the side of the road.

"We have another daughter, my love." His emotion was unstoppable this time, his voice breaking over the endearment.

"Of course you were right," Emmaline's voice held humor and love, despite her ordeal.

"We have nothing to cut the cord," Fanny said softly, half in question and half in worry.

"I know," Emmaline said. "Swaddle her, and I'll carry her back to the house. Lionel promised we were close."

"I didn't *promise*," he said, unable to stop staring at his daughter even as Fanny began to wrap her in the too-large blanket. Lionel pulled off his coat and used it to swaddle her instead.

"We aren't far," David said softly. "How can I help?"

"We need to get them into the cart—together." He held their daughter toward Emmaline. "Ready?"

She nodded and took the babe, her lips curling into a smile. "She's so beautiful."

"Just like her mother. I'm going to lift you both into the cart." Lionel looked to David. "Can you arrange a place for her on the floor, preferably with blankets?"

"We'll do our best." David clapped a hand on Lionel's shoulder before returning to the cart.

"I'll stand beside you and make sure you're secure," Fanny said before glancing at Lionel in question.

Lionel leaned forward and tucked a blonde curl behind his wife's ear before kissing her cheek. "Hold on to our daughter. I've got you. Or I will." He flashed her a smile of encouragement then got to his feet before squatting beside her.

It was awkward as hell, but he managed to lift them from the ground while Emmaline cradled the babe. He quickly carried them to the cart where David had arranged a sort of nest of blankets. David helped settle them into the vehicle.

Benedict, their golden-haired son, immediately sat next to Emmaline, his worried gaze taking in his mother and then his baby sister. "Are you all right, Mama?"

"I'm wonderful, my darling. Come and meet your new sister."

Another wave of emotion cascaded over Lionel as he climbed into the cart. He looked back to the groom who'd held Emmaline's hand. "Thank you. We'll send help for the repair as soon as we get back."

The groom waved, and once David and Fanny were resettled in the cart, they took off toward the house. Lionel situated himself behind Emmaline once more so she could rest against him. She held their daughter, whose face was just barely visible amidst Lionel's coat, and Benedict sat close next to them.

"Aren't you cold?" Emmaline asked Lionel.

"I am completely unaware of the temperature at the moment." In fact, he had been overheated.

"What's her name?" Benedict asked.

"She doesn't have one yet," Lionel said. "Do you have a suggestion?"

"Rose," Gray offered. "They smell nice."

"Not Caroline," Benedict said. "We already have one of those."

Lionel kept from laughing. "Yes, we do. That would be very confusing to have two."

"Like there are two Grahams," Gray said.

"But you are Gray, not Graham," Lionel reasoned.

"Perhaps we could call the baby Caro to differentiate."

Emmaline touched her daughter's nose. "Or we could call her Natalie since it's Christmas Eve."

"Perfect," Lionel said, smiling.

And then Natalie decided she'd had enough of looking serene and began to squall.

∼

Later that evening, Emmaline reclined on a chaise in the drawing room next to the fire, blazing with the Yule log, her newborn daughter asleep in her arms. This was not how she'd envisioned her Christmas Eve, and yet it was the best one she could remember.

"Only the Duchess of Danger would have a baby outside," West said, smiling, as he went about the room refilling drinks.

Fanny held up her empty glass for sherry. "I'd argue the Duchess of Daring would be more suited to such a thing. Or maybe the Duchess of Defiance."

"Oh, Lucy would absolutely give birth outside. In a tree perhaps," Ivy said of their friend, the Countess of Dartford, who was also known as the Duchess of Daring. It was from the silly nicknames Ivy and Lucy and their other friend Aquilla had started several years ago. They'd assigned faux dukedoms to men they dubbed the "untouchables." Lucy's husband was the "Duke of Daring," owing to his risky pursuits such as racing and riding in balloons. Of all the wives of the "dukes," Lucy had publicly adopted her husband's nickname—because she'd also adopted his thrill-seeking behavior. She was now as accomplished a racer as her husband.

Everyone laughed as Emmaline contemplated her husband—the Duke of Danger. Because of his past as a serial duelist. Thankfully, that *was* the past, for he hadn't dueled in years. She briefly thought of her former husband, who Lionel had killed in a duel that her husband had insisted on having. Lionel still harbored guilt about it and always would. They both did because without that duel, they wouldn't have married and fallen in love.

Life could be especially strange. Natalie snuffled in her lap. And wonderful.

Lionel came back to the chair he'd recently vacated to refill Emmaline's wassail. Sitting down beside her, he offered the cup, then took it back after she'd taken a sip.

"Thank you for taking such good care of me. Of us."

His blond brows twitched as he gave her a heart-stopping smile. "Thank you for being the most fearless woman I know."

"What was I supposed to do, fall to the ground and bemoan something that was completely out of my control?" she teased.

"You would never. You have met everything life has given you with poise, dignity, and an inimitable drive to not just survive, but *thrive*."

"It is easy with a partner who makes every day worth living—and loving."

Caroline toddled over to them and held her arms up for Lionel to put her on his lap. He did so without question and dropped a kiss on the top of her blonde head. Most of the children sat in the middle of the floor, playing with toys and chattering about the day. Leah had told them all of her and Jasper's adventure. Each time she shared the story—and Emmaline had heard it three times now—Jasper's tumble into the stream grew more dramatic. Rather, her *rescue* of him did.

"Shall we toast to the most memorable Christmas Eve on record?" West suggested.

"Hear, hear," David said.

West raised his glass. "To Leah and Jasper, for bringing unnecessary excitement to our Yule log hunt."

Leah stood and curtsied, which brought laughter from all quarters.

"And to my wife for her courage and, er, stamina." Lionel kissed her cheek.

Emmaline smiled down at their daughter. "To Natalie, for reminding us all how fortunate we are on this day of all days."

Everyone lifted their glasses and drank. Before Leah sat back down, she looked to West. "Papa, will you tell a story?"

West had been about to sit down next to Ivy on a wide settee. Instead, he set his glass on a table and rubbed his hands together. "Let me see... Have you all heard the story of the Fairy and the Toadstool?"

The children shook their heads and directed themselves toward him, instantly becoming a rapt audience.

"Once upon a time, there was a fairy who had to spend all of her time watching young fairies."

"Did they fall in streams?" Leah asked.

West narrowed his eyes at her briefly. "Shh. Don't interrupt. No, they didn't fall in streams. They liked to play among the toadstools, which to them were like a forest of trees."

"Did they choose one to be the Yule log?" Sebastian asked.

West turned to Ivy, who held Julia on her lap. "Notice the only children with ill manners are ours."

She looked up at him in exaggerated innocence. "I hope that's not a commentary on my mothering skills. They don't interrupt *me*."

Emmaline clapped her hand over her mouth to

stifle her laughter. Lionel grinned before sipping his port.

"No, they do not. You are, without a doubt, and I do apologize to our guests, the best mother." West looked back at his son and daughter and exhaled. "Pray, children, can you pretend I have at least a modicum of your mother's authority?"

Leah straightened her spine and elbowed her brother, who sat to her left. "Yes, Papa. We're sorry. We shan't interrupt again."

West wasn't sure he believed her, but he also wasn't sure he cared. He really was as soft as they came.

He went back to his story. "Butter—she's the fairy who had to watch the younger fairies—"

"Sorry, Papa, I have to ask, is the fairy's name really Butter?"

"Yes."

"But why?"

Before West could answer, Ivy broke in. "My darling, perhaps if you let Papa tell the story, you'll find out."

Sebastian laughed, and Leah pressed her lips together.

West smiled at his daughter and continued. "Butter had soft, yellow hair, like butter."

Leah grinned then opened her mouth, but then snapped it shut again.

"As I was saying," West said, "Butter had to watch the younger fairies because it was her job, and she was frightfully in need of money to pay for her room at a boarding house. She had no family or home of her own."

"Well, that's sad." Leah clapped her hand over her mouth.

"One day, a young fairy called Sparrow—and Leah, do *not* ask me about his name—told Butter there was a fairy trapped in one of the toadstools. Butter had never heard such a thing and assumed Sparrow was telling a tale. She asked where he'd heard such a thing. He answered that his older brother had said so and that it was absolutely, positively true.

"Butter was sure Sparrow's older brother was playing a jest and resolved to tell him to stop filling his younger brother's head with lies. When it was time for the fairies to go home, she accompanied young Sparrow, intent on speaking to his brother.

"Sparrow went into his house to fetch his brother but came out alone. 'I'm sorry, but Stone isn't at home,' he said to Butter. 'Perhaps you can try tomorrow.'

"Frustrated, Butter left. She went back the next day, but he still wasn't there. She went the next day and the day after that—every day for a week. She finally asked if he even lived there.

"'Of course he lives here,' Sparrow said. 'He's my brother.'

"'I'm beginning to think your brother is as fictional as the fairy trapped in a toadstool.'

"Sparrow shook his head. 'It's not fiction. Go and look closely at the toadstool with the gray spots on the stem.'

"'That is where I'll find the fairy trapped in the toadstool?' Butter asked.

"Sparrow nodded. 'Then you'll have to figure out how to set him free.'

"'The fairy is a he?' Butter asked. For some reason, she'd assumed it was a lady. A princess, perhaps.

"'So my brother says,' Sparrow said. 'He also said that if the fairy isn't set free before the full moon, he will be trapped forever.'

"Since the full moon was that night, Butter decided she'd better go—just so she could prove to Sparrow and his brother that there was no fairy.

"Armed with an axe so that she could cut into the toadstool if necessary, she went after dinner, arriving at the gray-spotted toadstool at twilight. She circled the toadstool, trying to determine how someone could be inside.

"'It just looks like a toadstool,' Butter grumbled. 'Sparrow lied, and I fell for it.'

"She turned to go, but from the corner of her eye, she saw a faint glow. It came from the toadstool—the center of the stem, actually. Pivoting slowly toward the toadstool, she noticed the light grew brighter.

"Butter went to the toadstool and put her hand on the smooth stem. 'Is someone in there?'

"A door opened at the base and out stepped the most handsome fairy she'd ever seen."

West's gaze connected with his wife's and Emmaline couldn't help but note the silent communication between them. It was flirtatious and loving and full of promise.

Emmaline looked over at Lionel and saw that he was watching her, his expression adoring. She reached over and took his hand.

West continued, "'Good evening, Butter. I am Stone.'

"'Sparrow's brother?' Butter wasn't sure she believed him. 'He said you were trapped, but clearly, you are not.'

"'Yes, that part was a fabrication. I needed to make sure you would come. I've spent this week inside the toadstool doing...things. Would you like to see?'"

The children had all leaned slightly forward, their attention fully on West's fantastical tale.

"Doubt made Butter hesitate," West said. "But curiosity won out, and she followed him inside. What she saw next made her jaw drop. It was a house. With furniture and even a hearth.

"'I was just about to light the fire—the first one,' Stone said. 'Would you like to sit in front of it with me?'

"Butter nodded, enchanted as she took in the coziness of the interior. There was a settee and an overstuffed chair perfect for reading. She could happily live there. But of course, it wasn't hers. It belonged to Stone. Or so she thought.

"'Is this your house then?' she asked.

"Stone turned from the fire and took her hand. 'No, I was hoping it would be yours. I know you don't have one.'

"Butter couldn't speak. She hadn't had a home of her own since she'd been very small, before her parents had died. 'You spent this week making a house...for me?'

"Stone nodded. 'Sparrow said you didn't have one. And now you do. There's a bedroom upstairs and another fireplace so you won't be cold.'

"Butter was sure she'd never feel cold again, especially when she looked into his warm, kind eyes. 'Thank you, Stone. Will you promise to visit?'

"He smiled at her. 'It would be my honor. Now, shall we have tea?'

"And they did."

The room fell silent. At last, Leah spoke. "What happened next?"

West hesitated. "Er, they drank their tea."

Leah frowned. "You said that. What about *after* the tea?"

"Ah, Stone left, and Butter went to bed."

"There has to be more," Leah said, squinting. ""Is that a real story, or did you just make it up?"

West chuckled. "All stories are made up by someone, my dear."

"And it was a very good one," Emmaline said. "You should write it down."

West appeared flattered. "Maybe I will."

"But it needs a proper ending, Papa," Leah insisted.

"And what kind of ending is that?" West asked.

"One with a happy ever after."

Emmaline looked to her husband once more and saw the laughter and love in his gaze. Her heart swelled in response.

"You're right," West agreed with his daughter. "Tomorrow, I shall share the happy ever after. Thanks to your mother, I know precisely what that means."

The adults in the room smiled and laughed, and the children began to chatter amongst themselves once more—until the butler came in, bearing a tray of marzipan. Then the children swarmed him.

Emmaline looked to their hosts. "Thank you, Ivy and West, for welcoming us this Christmas. It's such a joy to be together."

"And to have one more," Ivy said, glancing warmly toward Natalie.

"Next year, there will be at least one more," Fanny said, indicating her belly, which only barely revealed the bump of a babe.

Arabella snuggled closer into her husband's embrace on a small settee. "Two."

"Congratulations!" Lionel said. "Make sure you aren't outside when your time comes—either one of you." He winked at them.

Emmaline stroked Natalie's cheek. "Oh, I think it worked out fine."

"More than," Lionel agreed.

"Hmm, it appears to be our turn," West said softly to Ivy, but Emmaline caught it.

Apparently, Lionel heard him too for he grinned and said, "Go upstairs then."

West's eyes sparkled as he gazed at his wife. "I intend to."

Lionel laughed. "Always the Duke of Desire."

"Always," Ivy murmured.

THANK YOU!

Thank you so much for reading *The Bachelor Earl*. I hope you enjoyed it! Don't miss the rest of the Matchmaking Chronicles series. And grab The Untouchables twelve-book series, starting with The Forbidden Duke featuring Genie's stepson, Titus, Duke of Kendal!

Would you like to know when my next book is available and to hear about sales and deals? Sign up for my VIP newsletter at https://www.darcyburke. com/readergroup, follow me on social media:
Facebook: https://facebook.com/DarcyBurkeFans
Twitter at @darcyburke
Instagram at darcyburkeauthor
Pinterest at darcyburkewrite

And follow me on Bookbub to receive updates on pre-orders, new releases, and deals!

Need more Regency romance? Check out my other historical series:

The Untouchables: The Spitfire Society
Meet the smart, independent women who've decided they don't need Society's rules, their families' expectations, or, most importantly, a husband. But just because they don't need a man doesn't mean they might not *want* one...

The Untouchables: The Pretenders

Set in the captivating world of The Untouchables, follow the saga of a trio of siblings who excel at being something they're not. Can a dauntless Bow Street Runner, a devastated viscount, and a disillusioned Society miss unravel their secrets?

The Phoenix Club
Society's most exclusive invitation...

Welcome to the Phoenix Club, where London's most audacious, disreputable, and intriguing ladies and gentlemen find scandal, redemption, and second chances.

Wicked Dukes Club
Six books written by me and my BFF, NYT Bestselling Author Erica Ridley. Meet the unforgettable men of London's most notorious tavern, The Wicked Duke. Seductively handsome, with charm and wit to spare, one night with these rakes and rogues will never be enough...

Love is All Around
Heartwarming Regency-set retellings of classic Christmas stories (written after the Regency!) featuring a cozy village, three siblings, and the best gift of all: love.

Secrets and Scandals
Everyone has secrets and some of them are a scandal . . . six sexy, damaged heroes lose their hearts to strong, intelligent women in the glittering ballrooms and lush countryside of Regency England.

Legendary Rogues
Four intrepid heroines and adventurous heroes

embark on exciting quests across Regency England and Wales!
If you like contemporary romance, I hope you'll check out my Ribbon Ridge series available from Avon Impulse, and the continuation of Ribbon Ridge in So Hot.

I hope you'll consider leaving a review at your favorite online vendor or networking site!

I appreciate my readers so much. Thank you, thank you, *thank you*.

ALSO BY DARCY BURKE

Historical Romance

The Untouchables

The Bachelor Earl
The Forbidden Duke
The Duke of Daring
The Duke of Deception
The Duke of Desire
The Duke of Defiance
The Duke of Danger
The Duke of Ice
The Duke of Ruin
The Duke of Lies
The Duke of Seduction
The Duke of Kisses
The Duke of Distraction

The Untouchables: The Spitfire Society

Never Have I Ever with a Duke
A Duke is Never Enough
A Duke Will Never Do

The Untouchables: The Pretenders

A Secret Surrender
A Scandalous Bargain
A Rogue to Ruin

Love is All Around
(A Regency Holiday Trilogy)

The Red Hot Earl
The Gift of the Marquess
Joy to the Duke

Wicked Dukes Club

One Night for Seduction by Erica Ridley
One Night of Surrender by Darcy Burke
One Night of Passion by Erica Ridley
One Night of Scandal by Darcy Burke
One Night to Remember by Erica Ridley
One Night of Temptation by Darcy Burke

Secrets and Scandals

Her Wicked Ways
His Wicked Heart
To Seduce a Scoundrel
To Love a Thief (a novella)
Never Love a Scoundrel
Scoundrel Ever After

Legendary Rogues

The Legend of a Rogue (first available in A Very Highland
Holiday anthology, autumn 2020)
Lady of Desire
Romancing the Earl
Lord of Fortune
Captivating the Scoundrel

Contemporary Romance

Ribbon Ridge

Where the Heart Is (a prequel novella)
Only in My Dreams
Yours to Hold
When Love Happens
The Idea of You
When We Kiss
You're Still the One

Ribbon Ridge: So Hot

So Good
So Right
So Wrong

PRAISE FOR DARCY BURKE

The Untouchables: The Spitfire Society Series
NEVER HAVE I EVER WITH A DUKE

"Never have I ever given my heart so fast . . . an enticing addiction that stays on your mind and in your heart long after the story is through."

– *Hopeless Romantic*

'There was such a fabulous build-up to Arabella and Graham's first kiss that when they finally give in to it I wanted to high five somebody.'

– *DragonRose Books Galore Reviews*

A DUKE IS NEVER ENOUGH

"I loved Phoebe and Marcus! Whether as individuals or together, they are just wonderful on the page. Their banter was delightful, and watching two people who are determined not to start a relationship do exactly that was a whole lot of fun."

– *Becky on Books....and Quilts*

"I love the passion between Marcus and Phoebe and not just the steamy bedroom scenes they had, but the passionate nature of their relationship. Their feelings for each other went far past that of just the physical even if they didn't realize it."

– *DragonRose Books Galore Reviews*

meets the one man who might change her mind, only to find his painful past makes it impossible to love. A wonderfully emotional journey from attraction, to friendship, to a love that conquers all."

-Bronwen Evans, *USA Today* Bestselling Author

THE DUKE of DECEPTION

"...an enjoyable, well-paced story ... Ned and Aquilla are an engaging, well-matched couple – strong, caring and compassionate; and ...it's easy to believe that they will continue to be happy together long after the book is ended."

-All About Romance

"This is my favorite so far in the series! They had chemistry from the moment they met...their passion leaps off the pages."

-Sassy Book Lover

THE DUKE of DESIRE

"Masterfully written with great characterization...with a flourish toward characters, secrets, and romance... Must read addition to "The Untouchables" series!"

-My Book Addiction and More

"If you are looking for a truly endearing story about two people who take the path least travelled to find the other, with a side of 'YAH THAT'S HOT!' then this book is absolutely for you!"

THE DUKE of DEFIANCE

"This story was so beautifully written, and it hooked me from page one. I couldn't put the book down and just had to read it in one sitting even though it meant reading into the wee hours of the morning."

-Buried Under Romance

"I loved the Duke of Defiance! This is the kind of book you hate when it is over and I had to make myself stop reading just so I wouldn't have to leave the fun of Knighton's (aka Bran) and Joanna's story!"

-Behind Closed Doors Book Review

THE DUKE of DANGER

"The sparks fly between them right from the start... the HEA is certainly very hard-won, and well-deserved."

-All About Romance

"Another book hangover by Darcy! Every time I pick a favorite in this series, she tops it. The ending was perfect and made me want more."

-Sassy Book Lover

THE DUKE of ICE

"Each book gets better and better, and this novel was no exception. I think this one may be my fave yet! 5 out 5 for this reader!"

"An incredibly emotional story...I dare anyone to stop reading once the second half gets under way because this is intense!"

THE DUKE of RUIN

"This is a fast paced novel that held me until the last page."

" ...everything I could ask for in a historical romance... impossible to stop reading."

THE DUKE of LIES

"THE DUKE OF LIES is a work of genius! The characters are wonderfully complex, engaging; there is much mystery, and so many, many lies from so many people; I couldn't wait to see it all uncovered."

"..the epitome of romantic [with]...a bit of danger/action. The main characters are mature, fierce, passionate, and full of surprises. If you are a hopeless romantic and you love reading stories that'll leave you feeling like you're walking on clouds then you need to read this book or maybe even this entire series."

THE DUKE of SEDUCTION

"There were tears in my eyes for much of the last 10% of this book. So good!"

"An absolute joy to read... I always recommend Darcy!"

THE DUKE of KISSES

"Don't miss this magnificent read. It has some comedic fun, heartfelt relationships, heartbreaking moments, and horrifying danger."

"...my favorite story in the series. Fans of Regency romances will definitely enjoy this book."

THE DUKE of DISTRACTION

"Count on Burke to break a heart as only she can. This couple will get under the skin before they steal your heart."

"Darcy Burke never disappoints. Her storytelling is

just so magical and filled with passion. You will fall in love with the characters and the world she creates!"

-Teatime and Books

LOVE IS ALL AROUND SERIES

THE RED HOT EARL

"Ash and Bianca were such absolutely loveable characters who were perfect for one another and so deserving of love... an un-put-downable, sensitive, and beautiful romance with the perfect combination of heart and heat."

– Love at 1st Read

"Everyone loves a good underdog story and . . . Burke sets out to inspire the soul with a powerful tale of heartwarming proportions. Words fail me but emotions drown me in the most delightful way."

– Hopeless Romantic

THE GIFT OF THE MARQUESS
"This is a truly heartwarming and emotional story from beginning to end!"

– Sassy Booklover

"You could see how much they loved each other and watching them realizing their dreams was joyful to watch!!"

– Romance Junkie

JOY TO THE DUKE

"...I had to wonder how this author could possibly redeem and reform Calder. Never fear – his story was wonderfully written and his redemption was heartwarming."

– Flippin' Pages Book Reviews

"I think this may be my favorite in this series! We finally find out what turned Calder so cold and the extent of that will surprise you."

– Sassy Booklover

WICKED DUKES CLUB Series

ONE NIGHT OF SURRENDER

"Together, Burke and Ridley have crafted a de-lightful "world" with swoon-worthy men, whip-smart ladies, and the perfect amount of steam for this romance reader."

–Dream Come Review

"...Burke makes this wonderfully entertaining tale of fated lovers a great and rocky ride."

–The Reading Café

ONE NIGHT OF SCANDAL

"... a well-written, engaging romance that kept me on my toes from beginning to end."

–Keeper Bookshelf

"Oh lord I read this book in one sitting because I

was too invested."

–Beneath the Covers Blog

ONE NIGHT OF TEMPTATION

"One Night of Temptation is a reminder of why I continue to be a Darcy Burke fan. Burke doesn't write damsels in distress."

– Hopeless Romantic

"Darcy has done something I've not seen before and made the hero a rector and she now has me wanting more! Hugh is nothing like you expect him to be and you will love him the minute he winks."

– Sassy Booklover

SECRETS & SCANDALS SERIES

HER WICKED WAYS

"A bad girl heroine steals both the show and a high-wayman's heart in Darcy Burke's deliciously wicked debut."

–Courtney Milan, *NYT* Bestselling Author

"…fast paced, very sexy, with engaging characters."

–Smexybooks

HIS WICKED HEART

"Intense and intriguing. Cinderella meets *Fight Club*

in a historical romance packed with passion, action and secrets."

–Anna Campbell, *Seven Nights in a Rogue's Bed*

"A romance...to make you smile and sigh...a wonderful read!"

–*Rogues Under the Covers*

TO SEDUCE a SCOUNDREL

"Darcy Burke pulls no punches with this sexy, romantic page-turner. Sevrin and Philippa's story grabs you from the first scene and doesn't let go. *To Seduce a Scoundrel* is simply delicious!"

–Tessa Dare, *NYT* Bestselling Author

"I was captivated on the first page and didn't let go until this glorious book was finished!"

–*Romancing the Book*

TO LOVE a THIEF

"With refreshing circumstances surrounding both the hero and the heroine, a nice little mystery, and a touch of heat, this novella was a perfect way to pass the day."

–*The Romanceaholic*

"A refreshing read with a dash of danger and a little heat. For fans of honorable heroes and fun heroines who know what they want and take it."

NEVER LOVE a SCOUNDREL

"I loved the story of these two misfits thumbing their noses at society and finding love." Five stars.

–A Lust for Reading

"A nice mix of intrigue and passion...wonderfully complex characters, with flaws and quirks that will draw you in and steal your heart."

–BookTrib

SCOUNDREL EVER AFTER

"There is something so delicious about a bad boy, no matter what era he is from, and Ethan was definitely delicious."

-A Lust for Reading

"I loved the chemistry between the two main characters...Jagger/Ethan is not what he seems at all and neither is sweet society Miss Audrey. They are believably compatible."

-Confessions of a College Angel

LEGENDARY ROGUES SERIES

LADY of DESIRE

"A fast-paced mixture of adventure and romance, very much in the mould of *Romancing the Stone* or *Indiana Jones*."

"...gave me such a book hangover! ...addictive...one of the most entertaining stories I've read this year!"

ROMANCING the EARL

"Once again Darcy Burke takes an interesting story and...turns it into magic. An exceptionally well-written book."

"...A fast paced story that was exciting and interesting. This is a definite must add to your book lists!"

LORD of FORTUNE

"I don't think I know enough superlatives to describe this book! It is wonderfully, magically delicious. It sucked me in from the very first sentence and didn't turn me loose—not even at the end ..."

"If you love a deep, passionate romance with a bit of mystery, then this is the book for you!"
    -Teatime and Books

CAPTIVATING the SCOUNDREL

"I am in absolute awe of this story. Gideon and

Daphne stole all of my heart and then some. This book was such a delight to read."

-Beneath the Covers Blog

"Darcy knows how to end a series with a bang! Daphne and Gideon are a mix of enemies and allies turned lovers that will have you on the edge of your seat at every turn."

-Sassy Booklover

Contemporary Romance

RIBBON RIDGE SERIES

A contemporary family saga featuring the Archer family of sextuplets who return to their small Oregon wine country town to confront tragedy and find love...

The "multilayered plot keeps readers invested in the story line, and the explicit sensuality adds to the excitement that will have readers craving the next Ribbon Ridge offering."

-*Library Journal* Starred Review on YOURS TO HOLD

"Darcy Burke writes a uniquely touching and heart-warming series about the love, pain, and joys of family as well as the love that feeds your soul when you meet "the one."

-*The Many Faces of Romance*

I can't tell you how much I love this series. Each book gets better and better.

-Romancing the Readers

"Darcy Burke's Ribbon Ridge series is one of my all-time favorites. Fall in love with the Archer family, I know I did."

-Forever Book Lover

RIBBON RIDGE: SO HOT

SO GOOD

" ...worth the read with its well-written words, beautiful descriptions, and likeable characters...they are flirty, sexy and a match made in wine heaven."

-Harlequin Junkie Top Pick

"I absolutely love the characters in this book and the families. I honestly could not put it down and finished it in a day."

-Chin Up Mom

SO RIGHT

"This is another great story by Darcy Burke. Painting pictures with her words that make you want to sit and stare at them for hours. I love the banter between the characters and the general sense of fun and friendliness."

-The Ardent Reader

SO WRONG

ABOUT THE AUTHOR

Darcy Burke is the USA Today Bestselling Author of sexy, emotional historical and contemporary romance. Darcy wrote her first book at age 11, a happily ever after about a swan addicted to magic and the female swan who loved him, with exceedingly poor illustrations. Join her Reader Club newsletter at http://www.darcyburke.com/readerclub.

A native Oregonian, Darcy lives on the edge of wine country with her guitar-strumming husband, their two hilarious kids who seem to have inherited the writing gene. They're a crazy cat family with two Bengal cats, a small, fame-seeking cat named after a fruit, and an older rescue Maine Coon who is the master of chill and five a.m. serenading. In her "spare" time Darcy is a serial volunteer enrolled in a 12-step program where one learns to say "no," but she keeps having to start over. Her happy places are Disneyland and Labor Day weekend at the Gorge. Visit Darcy online at http://www.darcyburke.com and follow her on social media.